CW00828358

TOWN
OF SHADOWS

CARNIVAL OF TERROR SERIES
BOOK 3

IAN FORTEY
AND
RON RIPLEY

EDITED BY ANNE LAO
AND DAWN KLEMISH

ISBN: 979-8-89476-061-2
Copyright © 2024 by ScareStreet.com

All rights reserved. This book or any portion thereof may not be reproduced or used in any manner whatsoever without written permission from the publisher except for the use of brief quotations in a book review.

This is a work of fiction. Any resemblance to actual persons, living or dead, or actual events is purely coincidental.

ENTER THE REALM OF TERROR...

We'd like to take a moment to thank you for your support and invite you to join our VIP newsletter.

Dive deeper into the darkness with exclusive offers, early access to new releases, and bone-chilling deals when you sign up at www.ScareStreet.com.

Let the nightmares begin…

See you in the shadows,
Scare Street

PROLOGUE

"Burkitt Cemetery is in five hundred yards on your right."

Mitch stared at the road ahead. There was no turn in five hundred yards to the left or right. There was nothing but forest. There was definitely no cemetery, nor did he want to find one.

"Turn right, now," the GPS instructed.

He slowed the SUV down in case there was a hidden turn he was missing. There was not.

"Honey, please, can we stop listening to the GPS now?" Kristy asked.

Mitch looked at his wife and grinned.

"You don't want to visit Burkitt Cemetery?" he teased.

They had seen a sign for Burkitt some miles back and were hoping to find it to get some directions to Dover. Instead, the GPS had stopped working properly a half-hour earlier and continued to direct them to impossible places like roads where forests were and phantom cemeteries.

He felt like they were driving in circles along the back roads through the forest. It had been too long since they'd seen a town, a rest stop, or even a gas station.

"Are we going to be much longer?" his son, Jason, asked.

Mitch glanced at the rearview mirror. Jason was staring back at him while his older sister, Hailey, listened to music on her headphones and stared out the window.

"Can't be much longer, buddy," Mitch replied.

"There are no other cars," Hailey said then, removing her headphones. She had not spoken in at least forty-five minutes. She hadn't wanted to go on a trip to see their grandmother in Dover at all, so she'd been bitter since they left home.

"What other cars?" Mitch asked.

"*Any* cars," she replied. "Not a single car has passed us on any road in like an hour."

"We tried a shortcut, honey. This is a little off the beaten path."

"Not a single car, Dad. I've literally been watching out for them."

"What do you want me to say, honey? This is a very remote part of the state."

"More like the dark side of the moon." Hailey returned her attention out the window and replaced the headphones over her ears.

They drove on down the long, empty stretch of road bordered on either side by walls of trees.

"She's not wrong, Mitch," Kristy said softly. He glanced at his wife.

"What?"

"There hasn't been a single car on this road. How can no one drive down a road? The state's not that big, this isn't the desert or anything."

"It's… the woods. It's remote, and I thought it would be faster. I'm sorry," he grumbled.

She frowned and put a hand on his forearm.

"I'm not blaming you for anything. What I'm saying is, I think something weird is going on. Like this road is closed or something."

"There would have been a sign," he pointed out.

"Maybe kids stole it, or we missed the sign or something."

"Either way," Mitch said, "the road has to go somewhere. We'll find an exit, we'll find a town, whatever. You can only drive for so long in this country before something turns up."

"Now entering Burkitt," the GPS advised. The scenery outside had not changed at all. Trees and more trees.

The sky above was slightly overcast, and the day was cool. It should have been a good day for travel, and based on what Mitch had mapped on his phone, they should have saved forty minutes of highway driving with this shortcut. Now, they were nearly an hour late.

The road dipped low ahead, and as the SUV approached, they could see what lay ahead.

"Ha!" Mitch barked, feeling vindicated.

A town was laid out before them, still mostly obscured by the forest but clearly something, at long last. A place to get gas, to get a bite to eat, and finally get back on track to the interstate and Dover. They'd still make Grandma's place in plenty of time for dinner.

Mitch slowed down as they passed a quaint little "Welcome to Burkitt" sign and entered the town proper. It was a folksy little village, the sort he'd passed through a hundred times in the past without staying. People lined the sidewalks, traveling shop to shop on their main street.

"Why are strangers waving at us?" Jason asked as they went. Couples on the sidewalk smiled and waved at the family. Kristy waved back.

"Just a friendly small town," she told their son.

"Freaks," Hailey muttered.

There was no gas station on the way in, just a few shops like a hardware store, a shoe store, and a diner. Plenty more town lay ahead, but Mitch found himself slowing the car even more.

"You're kidding," he muttered.

"What?" Jason asked, leaning forward from the back. "Is that a tree?"

It was a tree. A fully grown, massive tree was growing in the center of the road. The pavement had cracked long ago to make room, and the thick, dark trunk rose high above the street, with widespread branches providing shade from one side of the road to the other. It was too large to drive past safely without jumping the curb onto the sidewalk in front of the little diner.

"I've never seen anything like that in my life," Kristy said.

Mitch had to agree; he'd never been to a town where traffic was stopped by a road tree.

"I guess we can get out here. Ask directions."

"I need to use a bathroom," Hailey said.

"Well, hold on, we can backtrack a little; there was a sideroad. I can go around the tree," Mitch added. He stopped the car and put it into reverse. Friendly townspeople strolled past them, waving, and saying hello.

The engine whined, and something clanked under the hood. The car sputtered and turned off.

"This is not happening," Hailey said from the back.

"Hold on," Mitch said, pressing the gas and hitting the ignition. There wasn't even a sputter. A faint, repetitive click came from under the hood, and nothing else.

"Honey?" Kristy said.

"It just needs a minute," he replied.

"It's not firing at all, Mitch. The starter's dead," she told him.

"It can't be dead, we were just..."

He tried again, and the same thing happened. After a moment, he closed his eyes.

"It's a town, honey. We made it to town. They'll have a garage or something somewhere. Let's just go look," Kristy said.

"Yeah," he agreed. "Yeah. There's got to be a mechanic."

He was no longer convinced they would get to his mother's place in time for dinner. The old woman was going to throw a fit.

"Okay," Mitch said, getting out of the car.

A few dozen locals were on the sidewalks, all smiling brightly and nodding or waving at him and his family.

"We'll just find a mechanic and get back on the road. We'll get there... today. Soon."

"There's a mechanic just up the road," an old man who had been listening in said, pointing past the tree toward nothing in particular.

"Okay, great, thanks," Mitch replied with a friendly nod.

"No problem, friend. He's right in the house on the hill; you can't miss it. Welcome to Burkitt."

Mitch nodded again and looked at his wife, who smiled.

"You take Jason, and I'll head into the diner with Hailey to use the restroom. I'll order you guys some lunch, and when you come back with the mechanic, we'll have it waiting, okay?"

"Hamburger, please!" Jason said.

"Hamburger," his mother confirmed, patting him on the head.

"Whatever. Let's just go," Hailey said, walking away from the others toward the diner. Kristy sighed and shook her head before giving her husband a quick kiss goodbye.

"Back in a few," he told her.

They split up, and one of the locals opened the door for Hailey to enter the diner, while Mitch put his hand on his son's back to give him a gentle push forward on the journey.

They passed the massive, bizarre tree and headed down the road. To the left and right were old houses, small businesses, a church, and a dentist. More tiny shops lined the way as the crowds thinned out.

The road led to a hill, as the man had told them, one that seemed to be the center of the village itself, with a massive, old house sitting atop it. The road came to a stop at the base of it, but it was still too far to know if it split to go around the hill or not.

Jason pointed out unique features on the surrounding buildings from old weathervanes to lawn ornaments to a strange topiary on one lawn as they walked. Fewer townspeople waved and said hello, and clouds rolled in overhead. It got darker the closer they got to the hill.

"Dad," Jason said quietly.

"Yeah?" he replied.

His son didn't answer. He looked down at the boy, whose gaze was fixed across the street. Mitch followed it. A man on the opposite sidewalk had stopped to watch them. He was older and stooped at the shoulders. His bald head had a large sore just above the ear, red and angry-looking, and he stared at them with wide, bloodshot eyes, and a manic smile.

"What's wrong with him?" the boy whispered.

"I don't know, son. Just ignore him," Mitch advised. They kept walking.

The sky darkened further, and a breeze picked up, rustling the leaves in the trees. Mitch's eyes wandered, and he saw that while there were fewer pedestrians on the sidewalks there were not fewer people. Faces in windows watched as they passed, some barely more than shadows. It was like the town had been alerted to their presence and everyone wanted to see them.

"Dad," Jason whispered again. Mitch put a hand on his son's shoulder.

"I know, buddy," he said. "It's okay. The people here are a little weird is all."

He glanced at a house and saw a face looking back from an upper window. He was certain the person had no lower jaw, but they faded into the shadows a moment later. He said nothing, not wanting to scare Jason any more than he already was.

Mitch looked back the way they had come. The road stretched far back, much farther than he thought they'd walked. He could barely see the tree behind them. How could they have walked so far?

"There he is!" Jason exclaimed.

Mitch looked forward once more and saw a man on the hill, in front of the house. He was an older man, wearing gray coveralls, working under the hood of a car from the sixties.

Mitch quickened the pace, heading toward the mechanic. The hill's incline was steeper than it looked, and he and Jason were forced to brace themselves carefully as they made their way up the hillside to what was probably the oldest house Mitch had ever seen, covered in long planks of dark wooden siding.

"Sir, hello!" Mitch said, approaching the mechanic.

The man lifted his head from the car's engine and glanced from Mitch to his son and back. He was older than Mitch had expected, at least in his sixties, with a long and serious face. His brown hair was short and neat and, despite working on a car, his hands were slender and perfectly clean.

"Hello," the mechanic said as he put his hands on his hips. He spoke with a British accent. "What can I do for you?"

"Our car died," Jason said. Mitch chuckled and shrugged.

"Yeah, we had an issue just inside town."

"Car died, huh," the mechanic said with a smile. "Isn't that something?"

"Yeah, I think maybe it's the starter."

The mechanic continued to nod and then extended his hand.

"You may call me Magister. Welcome to Burkitt," he said.

Mitch pursed his lips, reaching for the other man's hand.

"Magister?"

The man's hand was as cold as ice when they shook.

"That's it," he said.

"I'm Mitch, and this is my son Jason."

"And there's Kristy and Hailey up at the diner, too. Whole new family. That is just wonderful," Magister said, still nodding.

"How does he know Mom and Hailey?" Jason asked.

"What did you just say?" Mitch asked at the same time.

"I have been waiting for new residents. Burkitt needs new residents," Magister said.

He took a step forward and Mitch took Jason by the shoulder, pulling him away from the man as he backed away along the side of the house.

"We're just going to head back now, and I need you to stay here, okay?" Mitch said. He continued backing up until his heels hit something hard.

He looked down at wooden cellar doors set into the hillside at the base of the house. Magister smiled.

"I need *you* to stay *here*," Magister replied.

7

The cellar doors opened, and thick ropes of darkness lashed out like whips, snaring Mitch and his son. They moved with such speed he barely managed a scream.

CHAPTER 1
THE LONELY ROAD

Shane checked the clock on the dashboard and then looked at the fuel gauge. They'd have to stop to get gas before they reached Burkitt. Wallaceburg was their best bet, he thought. Closest stop to Burkitt, decent coffee at the diner. It would do.

"This all seems familiar but also not. Does that make sense?" Herbert asked.

Shane glanced at the ghost wedged into the passenger side of the car. Once billed as the Thousand-Pound Man in a sideshow, Herbert had probably weighed around four hundred pounds when he passed away. Not the biggest man in the world by a long shot, but sideshows exaggerated as a rule. Still, he was bigger than the seat, and if he were a living man, it would have been impossible for him to sit there.

"Yeah, I understand," Shane replied.

Really, they were in the middle of nowhere. The forests of Delaware were the same as the forests of pretty much everywhere in the Northeast. They could have been in Canada, even. But there was still that vague sense of familiarity.

Herbert had been there decades earlier, with the Bartolomy and Sons' Carnival and Sideshow. That was when all their trouble started. When a spirit from the town of Burkitt had killed two boys and framed the son of a former carnival worker turned ghost. When the boy, Dash, was killed by the Burkitt townspeople, his mother lost her mind.

Dash's death set into motion a decades-long quest for revenge that Shane had finally ended, with Herbert's help, at a children's hospital in

New York state. It was there they put a stop to the ghost of Lisette, the mother of the dead boy. But it was not enough.

Burkitt had started everything. The ghost from Burkitt killed the boys and set the townspeople on their murderous rampage that ended in the death of an innocent child. Shane had gone to Burkitt and found a true ghost town, abandoned by the living but full of more ghosts than should have been in one place.

Something was bad at the core of Burkitt, something that attracted dark spirits. Even a cemetery didn't have so many dead. And they were all dark and twisted in Burkitt. It wasn't natural.

Now that Lisette was destroyed, and he was no longer suspected of any of the murders she'd committed, Shane wanted to close the book on the whole story. They had to go back to where it all started.

"I wish the others could have been a part of this," the ghost said.

Before Lisette's rampage, the carnival had been a tight-knit group of living and dead. No one was left anymore, though. Only Herbert.

"It's enough that you can finish it," Shane told him. "For everyone. We'll make sure Burkitt can't do this again."

"You have a dark optimism," Herbert replied. "And confidence in your ability to face off against a nightmare and destroy it."

"Have you seen it fail yet?"

"No," Herbert said. "I suppose not."

For a ghost, Herbert was still very much like a living man. He was not aggressive, and even in a fight, he seemed to only want to do the bare minimum. Not that Shane expected anyone to fight for him, he had just never met a ghost as opposed to violence as Herbert seemed to be. He would have talked his way out of conflict if he could. With the living and with the dead.

Despite his preference for passivity, Herbert had proven he could be relied on in a pinch. He'd had Shane's back more than once already and had earned his trust. Shane needed someone to head into Burkitt with him, and Herbert was the best choice.

If it were a simple matter of finding and eliminating a single spirit, Shane would have headed to Burkitt alone and ended things. But there was nothing simple about Burkitt.

The little history he'd learned from the people of Wallaceburg painted a picture of a town that had rotted away to nothing. Deaths and disappearances had plagued the place for years. The town had finally folded sometime after Dash died, and anyone left alive had moved away. All that remained were ghosts. Too many ghosts.

Shane hoped that finding the spirit responsible wouldn't be too difficult. Herbert had seen it before, something that barely looked human, and he would know it when they found it. If any other ghosts in town caused trouble, they could meet the same fate.

The plan was not exactly detailed. "Find ghost and destroy ghost" was the whole of it. Shane hoped it would be that easy, but he was not foolish enough to pin any real expectations. Too many things smelled wrong about the place.

People nearby avoided the town. They had a sense that it was bad and kept away without being able to explain why. That, on its own, told Shane a lot.

In Nashua, his home had the same effect on the world around it. Birds didn't nest in the trees in his garden, and insects didn't burrow in the grass. The house exuded some energy or aura. It was haunted, and living things knew it.

Burkitt was the house on Berkley Street on a bigger scale. Not a haunted house, but a haunted town. It repelled the living and made them want to stay away. And that also meant it likely held surprises similar to Shane's home. Nothing was really as it seemed. The town was not exactly alive; neither was the house. But it still did things. It still wanted things.

What was eating at Shane was the why of it all. Dorothy, the owner of the diner in Wallaceburg, had told him that there were people in town who had never been to Burkitt but would never go there, either. They just knew to stay away.

He didn't know enough. He knew nothing about the spirit that had attacked the carnival and framed Lisette's son. Maybe it was just a rogue entity, a dark thing like those in Shane's cellar. Maybe all the spirits in town were acting on their own behalf and nothing was organized. Maybe it was just a confluence of chaos, a bunch of random, horrible events and accidents that created a perfect storm. He didn't know.

"We're almost there," Herbert said, pointing out a sign on the side of the road. They were seven miles from Wallaceburg. There was no mention of Burkitt at all, not that it mattered. Shane remembered the way.

The trees thinned out, and buildings soon filled in the gaps. A farm supply store, an actual farm, and a few random houses. They were within the town limits of Wallaceburg soon thereafter, and Shane kept to the glacial speed limit dictated by the signs, rolling past the bed-and-breakfast where he'd spent a night, and then the town library that was in a house not all that different from his own.

He pulled into a gas station across the street from the diner and filled the tank while Herbert joined him.

"Felt like stretching my legs," the ghost said.

Shane chuckled but said nothing. People went about their business in town, shopping or walking dogs or a hundred other things. If anyone in town cared that they were just a few miles from a ghost town, no one showed it. It was likely an out-of-sight, out-of-mind thing. To them, to a rational mind that didn't know better, it was just an abandoned town. Why would anyone give it a second thought?

Shane filled the tank and paid before driving his car across the street and parking it again.

"Diner?" Herbert asked.

"Good place to get info. And coffee," Shane pointed out.

"Undercover work?" the ghost asked.

Shane got out of the car and pulled a cigarette from his pack, lighting it and breathing in deeply before fixing Herbert with a judgmental look.

"Undercover what?"

"I don't know. This is on the down-low, isn't it? We're infiltrating a haunted town."

"No one cares," Shane told him as he walked closer to the diner doors. "It's not like a secret military base or anything."

"Have you ever broken into one of those?"

Shane took another puff and nodded.

"Yes. This will be a lot easier."

As they spoke, a dark blue truck with a yellow stripe came from the same direction they had come, speeding through town with red and blue lights flashing. Shane watched it go, catching the Delaware state police logo on the side of the vehicle as it passed. It was heading toward Burkitt.

Shane kept smoking with Herbert at his side. A second trooper, this time in a blue sedan, sped past as well.

"It's because you said it would be easy," Herbert said after both vehicles passed.

Shane nodded, finishing the cigarette, and pinching out the butt before fieldstripping it. There was no guarantee those troopers were heading toward Burkitt. But that was the road he'd traveled to Wallaceburg when he visited the first time, and it went straight there.

He opened the door of the diner and headed inside. Herbert followed him to a booth, and they sat facing each other, Shane with his back to the rear of the restaurant.

"Well, look what the cat dragged in," a familiar voice said. Dorothy set a mug on the table and held up a coffee pot. Shane grinned, and she filled it for him. "It's Shane, right?"

"Good memory," Shane said to the older woman.

"Couldn't get enough of the coffee here, am I right?"

"It's really good," he admitted.

She put her hand on her hip and gestured with the pot toward the window.

"You must be here for all the fuss then, huh?"

"What fuss?" Shane asked. Herbert, invisible to Dorothy, stayed silent and listened.

"Up in Burkitt. State police been swarming down there all morning looking for that missing family."

Shane glanced at Herbert and sipped his coffee again.

"Hadn't heard about it. What happened?"

"Mom, Dad, and two kids supposed to be on the way to Dover to visit Grandma. Guess they had one of them 'find my phone' tracker things, and all of them point to Burkitt, only cops couldn't find them in town, just the phones. Missing forty-eight hours now."

"Oh no," Herbert said quietly.

"The police haven't found anything yet?" Shane asked.

Dorothy looked at him consideringly and grunted before setting the coffee pot on the table and leaning in.

"You were there. Last time I met you, you'd just been there. Came in pretty banged up, as I recall. What do *you* think the cops found?"

Shane knew they'd find nothing if the town didn't want them to, but that left a lot of wiggle room.

"From what I'm hearing, they're having trouble getting anyone to enter the town," Dorothy added.

"They're afraid?" Shane asked.

She picked up the coffee pot and shrugged.

"Just a rumor I been hearing this morning. People saying they set up a blockade so no one can get out of town. No one's heading in, either. Told you… something about that place. You going to be ordering anything to eat?"

"Coffee's fine for now, thanks," Shane said.

"All right, give me a holler if you change your mind," she said, leaving the table.

Shane took another sip as she walked away while Herbert stared out the window.

"A whole family," he said.

"Haven't found them yet. Still might," Shane suggested. He didn't believe it, but it was possible. He was more concerned that there was now a police blockade between them and Burkitt. He had just gotten off the police radar.

Now he needed to find a way to sneak past them again.

CHAPTER 2
WAYFINDING

Shane finished his coffee. Three more state police vehicles passed during his time in the diner. He could only imagine what they were doing up the road. If the town repelled people, it was done so with feeling more often than not. The cops involved would have a gut instinct that something was wrong, but that was hardly enough for them to avoid an active investigation into a missing family.

Cops dealt with bad feelings all the time. Something else had to have happened in Burkitt to make the police fall back and create a barricade, if that was indeed what had happened. Of course, the locals in Wallaceburg would be left out of the loop on the details. The police were trying to keep something under wraps.

"Do you think the town killed some police?" Herbert asked, as though reading Shane's mind.

"Not openly," he replied.

Smart ghosts stayed hidden and worked in shadows. Just because a cop couldn't shoot a ghost didn't mean that the living couldn't cause problems for the dead, especially in a situation like this. Maybe the whole town of Burkitt would get bulldozed as a result.

Nothing suggested the ghosts in Burkitt were geniuses, but a haunted town had to do something to stay under the radar for so long. Unless things had changed. Maybe the missing family was a tipping point, and now the spirits didn't care. If that was the case, something could have happened to the police.

"Then what?" Herbert asked.

"Missing?" Shane suggested, keeping his voice down so as to not draw attention. "A few uniforms go in and don't come out. The rest get spooked and block the town because they can't find anything. Now, no one wants to go in, but they can't admit it. Seems cowardly. So, they're working on the idea that someone is in town. Crazed gunman, terrorist, whatever. Some excuse where the proper procedure is to stay outside the town limits."

"But then their men don't get rescued," Herbert pointed out. Shane shook his head.

"Not until backup arrives. They'd call in some big guns. SWAT, or something heavily armed and armored. They'll light Burkitt up once they feel they're strong enough."

"Then what happens to the family?"

"They'll try to find them. Save them. But if they are alive, and the ghost we're looking for has them, it'll use this as an opportunity. Put on a show, make a scene. It likes chaos, right?"

"From what I recall, yes," Herbert replied. The ghost turned a bunch of regular townspeople into a bloody revenge riot. It could do a lot worse with anxious, heavily armed police.

"We need to get in there before the police do anything rash," Herbert added.

"We do," Shane agreed. They needed another way into town, past the police barricade. They needed someone who knew about Burkitt.

Shane put money on the table and stood, giving Dorothy a quick wave across the room. She smiled and returned the gesture as he made his way back outside with Herbert.

"Do you have a plan?" the ghost wanted to know.

"Go to the library," Shane said. Louise, the town librarian, had a lot of local knowledge. She was also the only other person in town that Shane had really spoken to.

They walked down the street from the diner toward the massive house that served as Wallaceburg's library. In the light of day, the place looked a little more welcoming than it had when Shane first arrived. Louise was outside on the porch, sitting in a chair reading a book with a cup of tea on a table next to her. She watched Shane approach without saying anything until he reached the porch steps.

"Mr. Ryan, back so soon? Seems like our town has charmed you," she said, smiling over her book.

"It's true; I couldn't stay away."

"At least you came during daylight hours this time."

"Trying to be considerate," he explained. Herbert said nothing and inspected the garden instead while Shane gestured down the street. "Seen what's happening today?"

"I have seen some police," she confirmed. "Something to do with you?"

"No. Something in my way."

Louise's eyes narrowed. Her bird-like features looked even more prominent in the light of day. She reached for her tea and held it in both hands as though savoring the warmth.

"Of course," she said. "You want to go back to Burkitt."

"I do," Shane replied.

She sipped from the cup.

"Does this have something to do with Daschel Hooks?"

Herbert perked up then, returning his attention to the conversation.

"She knows about Dash?" the ghost asked. Shane ignored him.

"In a roundabout way," Shane told her.

"That's a bit vague, don't you think?"

Shane smiled and nodded, looking back down the road toward Burkitt. It was much too far to see from the library, but it was waiting out there.

"It has to do with why I was here before. What I was researching."

"Murder," Louise said. "The murder of someone from Burkitt."

"It ended up being several people."

Louise frowned and took another long sip of her tea, cradling the mug and looking into it.

"Is a murderer hiding in Burkitt?"

She meant something different from what Shane meant, but he nodded.

"I think so."

"And the family that went missing two days ago, are they involved?"

"Perhaps," Shane said honestly. "I need to get into the town. But I think the state police ran into something that got them spooked and made them set up a barricade. Now I have to find a way around them."

"You want to sneak past a police barricade," she clarified.

"I do," he told her.

"And so you came to the town librarian."

They stared at each other for a moment and Shane had to smile.

"I came to someone who could tell me what I need to know."

Louise set down her tea.

"Last time you wanted information about the past, morbid though it was. And I know some local history, and I was happy to share that. Even with a stranger. But now? What do you need this information for, Mr. Ryan? What good can come from you sneaking past police instead of going to them with your concerns?"

She was very serious in her question, and her tone was sharp. Shane hoped there could be some playfulness, some sense of mystery that would allow him to push past any suspicion she might have. That was not the case.

"I do not believe the police are equipped to handle what's waiting for them in Burkitt," he answered.

She had to have known the same stories that Dorothy at the diner knew. She had to have heard rumors and know that not only did everyone in town avoid Burkitt, but for the same unspoken reasons.

People out in the "real world" liked the comfort of things being predictable and explainable. A million people owned Ouija boards, or talked to psychics, or were afraid of dark shadows in their attics. But nearly all of them were happy to turn on a light and make all that scary stuff go away. They all needed the comfort of a feeling that, deep down, none of it was real. Or harmful.

Ghosts were like lions to most people, at least that was how it seemed to Shane. Terrifying, deadly, and maybe even something they'd seen in person. But behind glass walls. From afar. The reality and nature of a lion was not something people wanted to deal with. Ever.

"What is waiting for them in Burkitt?" Louise asked softly.

"A murderer," he answered simply, taking them full circle. But he knew it wasn't enough. She wanted to know why it was his job to stop the killer. Why him and not the police?

"There's something in Burkitt that has been there for a long time."

Shane knew it was a fine line to walk. He was not inclined to let relative strangers know what he did. Most people would think he was lying, or insane, or a mix of both. Louise struck him as a practical and intelligent woman. But she was also a woman who knew things. She could read between the lines easily enough.

"There's nothing in Burkitt, Mr. Ryan. The town was abandoned years ago. Nothing lives there anymore."

"No. Nothing lives there anymore," he repeated.

She stared at him, and he could see her breathing quicken. Her posture had become stiffer. She was anxious.

Nervous may be a better word.

"This missing family. The police have to be able to find them," she insisted.

"I heard they pulled back. That's just what I heard in town," he said.

"I heard that as well," she agreed.

"They pulled back, and to me, that means something scared them.

And when they regroup, it's going to be from a place of fear."

She was sitting on the fence, and he could see it. She knew the stories about Burkitt. Maybe she had even gone there once and felt the negative energy. Whatever the case, she both did and didn't want to believe there was something there. Something to fear.

"Give her my cameo," Herbert suggested.

Shane glanced at him, not wanting to speak.

"Trust me," the ghost urged.

Shane reached into his pocket and pulled out the tiny, cloth-wrapped bundle that held the old cameo necklace. It was Herbert's item, the haunted relic of his past that bound his ghost to the world. Where it went, so did he.

Shane kept it with him since they'd met, making Herbert his *de facto* partner as they pursued Lisette. But he kept it wrapped in a cloth as well. The item was ice cold, the same as all haunted things, and even someone who couldn't see ghosts would feel it.

"Would you take a look at this?" Shane asked, holding it out for her. Herbert moved closer so that he was right at Shane's side.

"A necklace?" she asked.

"Yes," he said.

She took it and gasped. The feeling of cold would have been a shock. Haunted items were not just cold but biting. They would become painful to hold in your bare hand in just a short time.

"What on Earth—" she began, cutting herself off with a scream as her eyes shifted from Shane to Herbert.

Louise pulled her hands back, dropping the cameo as she covered her mouth, eyes wide with fear.

"Don't be scared," Herbert said softly, raising his hands.

The old woman's face had drained of color and Shane feared for a moment her heart was going to give out.

"You're Herbert Buck!" she gasped. Herbert smiled a genuine smile and looked at Shane with an expression caught somewhere between delight and confusion.

"You know him?" Shane asked.

Louise was frozen, staring in astonishment. Shane retrieved the cameo, wrapped it, and placed it in his pocket once more.

"I saw your photo in a book. From the Bartolomy sideshow. It was a photo of you at Navy Pier…"

"Oh," Herbert said, chuckling. "I remember that. That was just after the war."

"You died…"

"I did."

"They called you the Thousand-Pound Man. The Fattest Man in the World. I always felt bad… for you."

Herbert laughed warmly.

"I appreciate your concern, ma'am. It was just my character. Helped me make a decent living."

"He's very proud of it, trust me," Shane added. Herbert had brought it up before and was adamant that he had not been exploited.

"You're a spirit," she said. She looked around, at the townspeople passing by on sidewalks, and cars going about their business in broad daylight. No one was any the wiser.

"Yes. I'm bound to that cameo. That cold is an… affectation, you might call it."

Louise looked at Shane then, a comprehension of dread on her face.

"You're not a madman, are you, Mr. Ryan? You think there's a ghost in Burkitt. A dangerous one."

"No, Louise," Shane replied. "I *know* there is. I've seen them there, and the police cannot handle them. But me and Herbert? Maybe we can. Better than cops with guns blazing."

Shane would not have been so quick to drop all their secrets on Louise, but it was Herbert's choice if he wanted to reveal himself to someone. And it looked like it was working.

"I can show you some old hunting roads. Paths through the woods that have mostly grown over, but they can get you into town, past the state police," the librarian told them. "Come inside."

CHAPTER 3

INFILTRATION

Louise could not take her eyes off Herbert. He smiled politely but seemed to be feeling awkward under her scrutiny. She marveled at his ability to be in the room but not in the room at the same time, how his bulk could pass through narrow doorways and fit in places it had no business fitting. Shane could tell she desperately wanted to touch him but was too polite to bring it up.

She had gone through some drawers in the library and come up with a map of the area that was produced by the Burkitt Chamber of Commerce sometime in the 1950s. It was very rudimentary and almost childish in its execution, but it showed most of the landmarks and roads. That included some hunting cabins and the roads she had mentioned, off the main road and hidden in the forest.

"You know," Louise began as Shane studied the map for their easiest point of access, "I had an aunt from Burkitt."

"Did she get out of town before things got bad?" Herbert asked.

"Oh, no, dear. The last time I saw her was at her funeral. I was in my teens then. We went to the funeral in Burkitt, and back in those days, it was as busy a town as Wallaceburg is. It had its misfortunes, the flu outbreak, a food poisoning scandal at a church bake sale, and things of that nature. But we never suspected..."

"I understand," Herbert said. She smiled at him.

"Anyway, my point. At her funeral, I saw a man in the cemetery, and he saw me. I felt silly telling my parents afterward. There were many people there, but I knew he was looking only at me. And he was not... not a real man."

She looked at Herbert, and her expression became awkward.

"Not to say you're not a real man, it's just—"

"I understand," he said reassuringly. "The man you saw was a ghost."

"I think so. But not like you. This one was menacing in a way I could not describe. He didn't attack me or threaten me in any way. It was only the look of him. This feeling, an overwhelming feeling of... terror. Had I been there alone, I know I would not have left alive."

"Some spirits can be very... bad," Herbert said, struggling for the word.

"But not all?"

"Not all," Shane offered, still studying the map.

"Then what happened in Burkitt? Is this all related? The carnival? The boys and Daschel? And now this family?"

"Yes," Herbert answered. "Burkitt is at the core of all these things. But we are hoping to put an end to it. If we can."

"An end to at least the ghost that killed those boys," Shane corrected.

There were many spirits in Burkitt, and it was not practical to assume they would have a chance to confront most of them. Not that he even wanted to. The more under the radar they could go, the better. Even more reason to use one of the hunting trails on Louise's map.

"I think this will work," Shane decided, holding up the map. "It's basic, but it'll do. There's at least one trail that should be easy enough to access without police seeing us. We need to avoid them but also what's waiting in Burkitt, so this takes some planning and guesswork."

"Are there... weapons? Things you need to protect you?" Louise asked, genuine concern in her voice.

"I have Shane," Herbert answered, and Shane tried not to laugh.

"We'll manage. Thank you for the map. We need to get going, though. Take advantage of daylight for as long as we still have some."

"Yes, of course," Louise said, still fascinated by Herbert. He paused and held out a hand for her as though to shake. She hesitated and then extended her own. Once more, she gasped as the cold of Herbert's ghostly flesh touched her own. Her hand passed through his, and the chill ran through her.

Louise flinched, and for a moment she looked as though she might pull away, but then she lifted her hand and ran her fingers across his broad chest, the tips dipping into his body.

"Remarkable," she whispered.

Herbert turned away from her and followed Shane out onto the porch. Louise followed as far as the door and then stopped. Another state trooper sped past the library, heading toward Burkitt.

"I trust you'll be careful," she said to them.

"I'm always careful," Shane assured her.

"And if you need me again… I'll be here."

"Thank you, Louise," Shane said.

"Yes, thank you, ma'am," Herbert echoed.

"I should thank you, Mr. Buck. This has been an illuminating visit."

Shane continued down the pathway to the sidewalk and then turned toward his car. Louise watched them go but Shane did not look back, though he caught Herbert turning to wave at least once.

"Little old for you, isn't she, Herbert?" Shane joked.

"That's not funny," Herbert replied. "She reminds me of my mother."

"Ahh," Shane said. "Well, you certainly impressed her. Risky move, mind you."

"You think so? She had kind but intelligent eyes. I trusted my gut."

"So you did, and it paid off," Shane said, holding up the map as they approached the car.

The path into Burkitt was going to involve a hike, but if they found the road in the woods, it would be a straight shot past what the police would have eyes on and right into the town proper.

They got into the car, and Shane headed slowly out of town, along the road to Burkitt. There were at least a handful of sideroads between Wallaceburg and their destination, so there was no reason for anyone to be suspicious of one more car heading in that direction. But Shane didn't know how far back the police held their line, and he needed to make sure they were out of sight.

Agent Xander Ventura had done him a favor by getting him off the police radar only a short time earlier. Shane might no longer have been wanted for multiple murders, but it didn't mean that the police from Delaware wouldn't have all seen his photo in the past week. If they were already out of sorts because of something that happened in Burkitt, Shane could become an easy target.

There were no other cars on the road out of Wallaceburg, and when they caught sight of the police blockade on the road ahead, Shane stopped the car and backtracked to the nearest side road.

"Guess this is our stop," he told Herbert as he pulled off and headed down a secluded, unpaved road bordered by fir trees. He drove until he could no longer see the main road and then pulled to the shoulder, keeping the car out of sight as much as possible.

They left the car and Shane paused for a moment, heading to the trunk to see if he had anything on hand that might be helpful. The iron rings in his pockets were a familiar standby and a reliable tool, but he was concerned that Burkitt might have a few more tricks up its sleeves.

"What are you looking for?" Herbert asked, joining him at the rear of the car.

The trunk was mostly empty save for some salt and bags he'd had on hand for months after a job in which he needed to stash a few haunted items on the fly. There was little in the way of weapons, except for a single bag he recognized as a gift from James Moran at one point.

"This," Shane said, lifting the small bag of iron filings. It wasn't much, but it was the only other weapon he had on hand. For emergencies.

"Are those... metal bits?" Herbert asked.

"Iron," Shane confirmed. The ghost nodded.

"Well, thank God for that," he said.

Shane laughed and closed the trunk before slipping the bag into his pocket.

"You'll be thanking me if we ever need it," he said, before pulling out the map once more while Herbert read over his shoulder.

"Downtown strip. The Old Fishing Hole?" the ghost said, reading sites that were prominently listed.

"Looks like it was a town tourism thing," Shane said. "But it matches what I remember of the town. Sunset Grill. Police station. Magister's House. All of this looks like what I remember from being there."

"Johnny's Scrapyard," Herbert remarked. It occupied a squarish plot of land on the map. "Bet that's haunted."

"Whole town is haunted," Shane reminded him, pointing toward the far end of the map. "But this is where we're headed. Blake Hunting Shack. That road goes into the fishing pond and the town on the other side. Right past the cops and anything they could hope to see from where they're set up."

"Good. Okay," Herbert said, looking at the woods. "Back to the forest."

They had already hiked through the woods to escape the FBI and searched through wooded areas around the carnival when Lisette was still murdering Burkitt citizens. It had become a hallmark of their time together.

Shane led the way, hoping the map scale was fairly accurate. They would need to travel at least two miles through the forest before they found the shack, and then the rest of the trip should be an easy walk down the road. He was taking all that on faith, however. The map was quite old.

Herbert moved silently but stayed at Shane's side as dead leaves crunched underfoot. He could move quietly if he needed to, but he was more concerned with speed and not losing daylight out in the woods. It was bright enough that he would have seen anyone trying to get the drop on him, anyway.

As they walked, Herbert's nervous habit of chatting about anything and everything bubbled to the surface. He told Shane about his mother, about the last time he'd visited a library, and about the one time he'd gone hunting with Bartolomy many years earlier.

"You ever notice that you have a story about everything?" Shane asked at one point.

"I do?"

"You do," Shane confirmed.

It wasn't a criticism, just an observation. Herbert had experienced more than most ghosts Shane had met, given that he had spent years traveling the country with a carnival. It was very different from how most ghosts exist. Being rooted to a haunted item meant travel was almost unheard of. Herbert's afterlife had been quite unique.

"Do you want me to stop?" Herbert asked unsurely.

Shane produced a pack of Lucky Strike from inside his jacket and shook his head.

"No. Just interesting to see a ghost engage in nervous chatter," he said, lighting a cigarette.

"Not used to cloak-and-dagger operations is all," Herbert explained. "My life was not very exciting before I met you."

"Do you wish you hadn't?"

They walked in silence for a moment while Herbert mulled over the question.

"Yes and no. I wish the circumstances that led you to the carnival never happened. But I do not regret meeting you and coming with you to put an end to this."

"Makes sense," Shane said. He checked the map again and then his watch. They'd be near the cabin soon if they were on the right track.

"You meet a lot of ghosts," Herbert said then, and Shane nodded.

29

"Are many of them like me?"

"Like you, how?"

"I feel like I'm the same man I was when I was alive. But then I think of Lisette, and the thing that killed those boys, or the children in the hospital… even Nils. They all went bad. They became monsters."

"Not all ghosts are monsters," Shane assured him. Herbert's expression did not indicate the answer had mollified him.

"Most?" he asked.

"A lot are," Shane said honestly. "You're definitely an outlier, Herbert. A lot of ghosts come back angry and resentful and looking to hurt people."

"But why?"

It was a question Shane was not in a position to answer. If anything, Herbert had the greater insight. He was dead. If he didn't have a better understanding of that crossover from life to death, Shane certainly wouldn't.

"I don't know, Herbert," Shane replied.

He also didn't have a lot of spare time to think about it just then. Ahead of them and to the right, through the trees, he could make out the small hunting shack they were looking for.

Shane stopped and signaled for the ghost to do the same. He finished his cigarette and stripped down the butt while he watched the building. There was no sign of anyone living or dead outside. The police hadn't found it, but that didn't mean nothing was lying in wait.

The shack was not big enough to be called a cabin, and had a door and a single window, as well as a small chimney. It looked very much crudely made, and probably extremely old, judging by the look of the wood that had been used. It also seemed abandoned. Dirt and detritus had built up outside until the base of the door vanished. The window was smeared with a layer of dust. Moss had reclaimed most of the exterior and it looked almost like it was a living thing.

"See anything?" Shane asked. Herbert shook his head.

"Not yet," he said.

They would have to approach. The road to town waited on the other side.

CHAPTER 4
HUNTER

"We'll have to find a way around the pond, but there must at least be a footpath or something," Shane said, showing the map to Herbert.

The fishing pond awaited at the end of the road. The map didn't show any path between the road and the town proper, but if someone had bothered to make a road to the hunting cabin, it couldn't just come out of the water.

They stood on the far side of the shack while Shane lit another cigarette. Once they got past the pond, they'd be deep in the heart of Burkitt, and likely beyond what the police were able to see.

Shane hoped they could find either the ghost they were searching for or the missing family before anyone had an idea someone else was in town. Once the job was done, it wouldn't matter if the state police found them. He just wanted them to stay out of the way until he was ready for them.

"There's a road," a man's voice said.

Shane turned swiftly, surprised by the presence of a new spirit only a few feet away. He stood in the shadow of the hunting cabin and had been looking over Shane's shoulder at the map.

"It's on the east side. There," the ghost said, gesturing with his finger. Shane didn't bother looking at the map.

"Not polite to read over a stranger's shoulder," Herbert pointed out.

The spirit laughed. Shane guessed the man was in his thirties. Scruffy looking, with a beard like a Brillo pad and hair sticking out from under a lopsided black knit cap on his head. His left eye was a muddy green, but his right eye was gone, a ragged and bloody hole where it once was. Shane could see the cabin behind him through the hole in his head.

"Heard you talking out here was all, thought I could offer a hand. Never seen a man hiking the woods with a ghost before."

"You know Burkitt?" Shane asked.

"Sure. Lived there all my life. And then some." The ghost gestured up and down his body.

"You know the ghosts in town?"

The ghost grinned and rubbed a hand through his ghostly scruff. He wore a pair of camouflage pants and a matching jacket, undone to show a white shirt beneath. A hunter. Not a good one from the look of his face, though. Shane was certain it was a bullet hole.

"You a ghost hunter?" he asked Shane.

"Just looking for one in particular."

"White skin. Red eyes. Moves like an animal instead of a man," Herbert added.

"Yeaaaah," the hunter said, looking Herbert up and down. "Boy, look at the size of you."

"Do you know it?" Herbert asked.

"Sure, I know that one. Real nasty piece of work. If I were you, I'd steer clear."

"Well, we need to see him," Shane said.

The hunter ghost chewed on his lip and kept his eyes on Herbert, grinning humorlessly.

"I used to know this girl in town named Patrice, and I tell you, I thought she was fat. I mean, she was fat; don't get me wrong. But boy, looking at you, it's like I never even knew what fat was before. Patrice was like Cheryl Tiegs next to you, big fella."

Herbert kept his poise while the hunter laughed and looked at Shane as though hoping he'd join in.

"Well, we'll just be heading into town then," Shane said.

"Oh, c'mon. Don't be so sensitive," the hunter said mockingly. "You know I'm just teasing, right, Big Boy?"

"Whatever you say," Herbert said, turning to walk down the road.

"You city folk, I swear," the ghost said.

Shane ignored him and headed toward the pond. He'd seen where the ghost had indicated there was a road. That was good enough.

They walked several yards before Herbert finally looked back.

"He's gone," he said.

Shane shrugged.

"Probably had to get back to making moonshine," he replied.

They continued down the hunting road, sheltered amid the thick tree cover, and around a bend toward the pond. Shane stopped as they cleared the curve, prompting Herbert to do the same. The hunter ghost waited on the path ahead of them, the same humorless grin on his face.

"You didn't need to run off all quick like that," the ghost said. He was a dozen paces in front of them in the center of the path, light streaming through the treetops and through the hole in his head.

"Didn't," Shane countered. "Just walked."

"Potato, potato," the ghost said, pronouncing the word the same each time.

"Looks like you're in our way," Shane pointed out. "If you wouldn't mind moving."

The hunter chuckled and shook his head.

"It's been a long time since anyone came out this way, you know that? I mean… I don't even know how long. Time gets away from you out here. But years, I know that. Been through a lot of winters. Lot of thaws. Eventually, you know, it's like you've always been alone out here."

"That'll happen when you're dead," Shane assured him. "We need to go."

"Oh, sure," the hunter said, stepping to one side. "I'm not out here to keep folks away. Not some guard dog at the fence."

34

Shane watched him as he walked past, expecting the spirit to make some kind of move, but he did not. The ghost watched as he and Herbert passed, then returned to the center of the dirt road.

"I don't keep people out," the ghost reiterated to their backs as they walked. "That's not what Magister needs me for."

Shane paused, removing the cigarette from his mouth as he looked at Herbert, then back at the hunter.

"The Magister?" he asked.

"He keeps me here to make sure no one leaves. No one's tried that, either. At least not down my way. But I gotta tell you, I've been here for so long, I think I need to shake up my duties a bit, you know?"

"I don't," Shane admitted.

The ghost's tone had become more serious and his voice flatter. He stared at Shane with murderous intent in his one eye, so his meaning was clear enough. Didn't hurt to string him along a bit, though.

"Who is the Magister?" Herbert asked.

"No one you need worry about, Big Boy. Unless he wants you to, I guess. He's kind of a collector these days, you could say. Been expanding the farm or whatever you want to call it. Branching out. But you'd need to follow the rules, and you look like the kind of fella who's not good with self-control."

"You'd be surprised," Herbert replied. There was a threat in his voice that the hunter didn't realize.

"Doubt it. But you, Baldy, I'm going to take for myself. Been so long since I got to hurt anyone out here, and I'm due for some fun."

Shane took a long puff on his cigarette, nodding to himself as he did so.

"Got it, sure. So, just to be clear... you're saying you want to fight?"

"I'm saying I think I'm gonna make Big Boy watch while I pull your spine out through your backside."

"Why would I watch that?" Herbert asked seriously.

Shane laughed, and the hunter's face twisted with anger. He had been restraining himself, it seemed. The ghost rushed Shane, arms extended like some clumsy horror movie monster from the fifties.

Like too many other spirits, the hunter had grown complacent over the years. He did not know how to fight because he never had to fight. He could just sneak up unseen and kill to get his thrills. He was a hunter after all. But, again, he was not a good hunter.

Herbert took a step back and Shane let the map fall to the side of the road where it would be out of their way. When the ghost was within reach, he took him by the wrist in one hand and used his momentum to pull him to the side. The ghost grunted while Shane stepped out of his way and followed through with a punch to the back of the head with his free hand.

The hunter stumbled, caught off guard by Shane's ability to touch him, and was too slow to recover. Shane's fist came down on the back of his skull into the hole that let the light through his eye socket.

Shane could see now that the ghost had been shot with a high-caliber weapon. The rear of his skull was blown away completely, and Shane's fist plunged into the bloody chasm. Flesh and brain squelched, and Herbert gasped audibly as Shane and ghost went to the ground, Shane's hand caught in the hunter's skull in a way that threw them both off balance.

They landed hard, Shane on his knees over the ghost who was face-down in the dirt. Half of his work was already done, so Shane capitalized on his unexpected advantage. He usually had to work a bit harder to destroy a spirit's skull.

The hunter thrashed to get up while pulling away from Shane's hand. Shane doubled down and pushed. His body weight behind him, his hand sunk through the ghost's skull until he could feel the earth through the hole where the spirit's eye had once been. He hooked two fingers through the hole like he was trying to grasp a bowling ball and pulled, using his free hand to hold the ghost in place.

The hunter wailed, muffled by the ground, then growled like a beast until bone snapped, and Shane crushed his face inward. The spirit's head crumbled like a dropped egg.

Energy burst from the spirit's body. What was once the shape of a man dispersed like vapors caught in a gust and Shane was thrown back into Herbert, who awkwardly tried to catch him.

"Is it always so violent?" Herbert asked, lifting Shane with one large hand until he was on his feet. Shane brushed himself off and gave a half-shrug.

"Destroying a ghost? Kind of violent by definition."

"The... explosion. Is there always an explosion?"

"It's explosive," Shane confirmed.

"But what is it? Why does a spirit explode?"

Shane chuckled again and retrieved the map from where he had dropped it.

"Honestly, Herbert, I don't know. I can't imagine anyone knows because no one comes back."

"It's permanent, though. It's death for the dead."

"Seems like it," Shane agreed.

"And a ghost can do it to another ghost." It wasn't a question.

Shane nodded again, looking Herbert in the eye. If Shane had to guess, his friend was already working on a plan. He was not vengeful, but Shane knew he had a hatred for the spirit that he had seen all those years ago. The ghost that had killed those boys.

"You have some kind of plan you're working on?"

"Just want to know what will happen when I find the ghost we're looking for," Herbert answered. He was being honest. Not really a bloodlust or desire for revenge. That wasn't Herbert's style. But a willingness to take care of business, at least.

"It's going to be interesting," Shane told him as they started back down the road.

CHAPTER 5
DROWNED MEN

The map was worse than Shane had expected. The fishing hole was not a pond as the map made it seem but a vast, swampy marsh. The water spread out among trees and drowned the road on which they walked. If there was a road as the hunter had said, Shane had no idea where to look for it. It was likely underwater as well.

Cattails and ferns dotted the landscape around the banks of the marsh, and the trees thinned out deeper in it, until they were spotty at best. Huge, skeletal trunks with bare branches rose from the still waters at irregular intervals.

From the edge of the water, Shane could see the town of Burkitt beyond the swamp. The house on the hill rose above all else, but other homes and buildings were scattered among the trees.

"There's a boat." Herbert pointed about thirty yards ahead of them to a half-sunken, ramshackle pier. Most of the wood was underwater, but an old rope tied to one of the posts was lashed to a floating rowboat. The swamp had grown considerably since it was moored there.

Shane sighed, not eager to get soaked but not convinced there was another way. The swamp looked large enough that navigating around it might have taken them well out of the way of town, maybe too close to the cops as well.

He pulled the pack of cigarettes from his pocket and held it above his head as he waded out. There was no telling how deep the water was, but he wasn't willing to risk wet cigarettes for anything.

Herbert glided across the top of the water, and he moved ahead as they got closer, pushing the boat toward Shane until it was at the end of the rope. He didn't have the dexterity to untie the knot holding it, but it was helpful, nonetheless. Shane was only up to his knees in water by the time he climbed in.

The inside of the boat was caked in old mud and dead leaves. The single oar was slightly warped but better than nothing. Shane sat and Herbert got in as well, his bulk not offsetting the balance at all but making him look remarkably silly in the small vessel.

"Ship's ahoy," Shane said, untying the mooring rope. He took up the weather-worn paddle and used it to push off on the bottom until the water was too deep to do so.

Navigating through the drowned trees was slow going until they reached the more open water. The trees there were much sparser and could be avoided, though he noticed more than one sunken stump that could damage the boat if they were not careful. Fortunately, there was no way the tiny boat and damaged oar were going to gain enough speed to cause serious harm.

The water smelled old in a way Shane had never experienced. Open water, out of doors, should not have such a smell. It was musty like a basement and reminded him of things that needed to be cleaned.

Herbert was oblivious to the smell, but like Shane, he was on edge. While Shane's eyes were locked on the far banks of the swamp and their destination, Herbert watched the water.

"Shane," he said once they were about a third of the way across the marsh. "Look."

He had not looked up at Shane when he spoke. His bulk was still seated, but he was leaning and staring straight down. Shane did the same, leaning to one side and looking into the water.

The murk was thick, but not so thick that it obscured everything. The water had a green cast and within it, several feet below the surface, the rotten and bloated face of a ghost stared up at the passing vessel.

More spirits came into view as the boat drifted. Many bore signs of having died in the water. Their wounds were pale and puckered, the flesh torn as though small creatures had nibbled down to the bone.

None of the spirits moved to the small boat, they simply watched it pass. Shane counted at least two dozen of them at the halfway mark. He started to see the skeletal remains at that point, the actual bodies that belonged to the dead. Some were caught on trees and other detritus, and it was clear they had been tied down, their ankles chained to rocks or sunken logs.

The lake was full of the spirits of murdered souls, men and women tied down and drowned in the swamp. He had never seen anything like it.

"How many are there?" Herbert asked.

Shane had no answer. He looked out across the marsh, the vastness of the water around them. It was no lake, not a great body of water by any means. But it was large enough. There was room for many dead, and he had seen dozens.

"Was this the ghost from Burkitt or something else?" Herbert wondered.

Again, Shane had no answer. There was not just one ghost from Burkitt, though Herbert's interest was only in the one who had killed the boys at the carnival. The spirits he had seen in Burkitt were deadly. And they had probably taken many lives.

The ghosts were from different eras, judging from the few details Shane could glean. Those that appeared as they had in life wore clothing that ranged from the fashions of the sixties to the turn of the previous century. There could have been a hundred years' worth of corpses in the pond. A century of death.

Shane thought of the things he had read at the library when he first got to Wallaceburg. The stories of the troubles Burkitt had faced. Disease outbreaks, economic downturns, missing people. Maybe the tragedies were masks; smokescreens to cover for greater losses. Maybe many of the people who supposedly left town for greener pastures had never left at all.

In the middle of the marsh, the water became too deep to make out anything clearly. There were still vague shapes and outlines, but bodies were lost in the darkness. A hand rose from the swamp and grasped the side of the boat. The fingers were skeletal, caked in mud and weeds.

Shane stopped paddling and waited. A second hand emerged, and the ghost pulled itself from the water. A head rose over the edge, only the barest scraps of dirty, pale flesh still clinging to it. The eye sockets were empty save for the mud that flowed from them like rivers of dark tears. The lower jaw still held flesh and still had a lip, but the upper part was stripped entirely.

The spirit pulled itself fully into the small boat, wedged between Shane and Herbert, the phantom mud pooling at its feet and spreading across the boat's bottom.

"You're making a mess," Shane told the ghost.

Other ghosts had gathered like swimmers in the water around the boat. They remained immersed yet closely packed like a school of sharks waiting for the first taste of blood in the water.

The ghost in the boat raised a hand and reached out. Shane was tense and ready, but the ghost did not reach for him at all. Instead, it extended its arm past his head and pointed to the shore from which they'd come.

"Go back," the ghost warned, its voice wet and popping.

"Already been there," Shane pointed out. "We need to get into Burkitt."

"No. Go back," the ghost said again. The mud was slowly filling the boat and forcing it lower in the water.

"We're looking for a spirit," Herbert said. "A pale thing with limbs like a spider and eyes like blood. It's from Burkitt."

"Go," some of the dead in the water said.

"Go back. Or die," the ghost on the boat warned.

"We need to get to Burkitt. Your warning has been noted," Shane said. "Now if you want to take your mud, we need to find that ghost."

"No," the ghost said again.

Shane sighed and laid the paddle in the bottom of the boat. Only inches separated him from the muddy spirit and while it hadn't been overtly aggressive, the edges of the boat were dipping low enough that they'd be taking on water in minutes if it didn't leave.

"Yes," Shane countered.

He moved quickly, taking the ghost by its collar in one hand and grabbing an exposed thigh bone in the other. The ghost was light and easier to move than he'd expected as he lifted and hurled it from the boat back into the swamp.

The phantom mud dissipated, and the boat's buoyancy increased, but the victory was short-lived. While many of the ghosts backed off, surprised by Shane's attack, not all followed suit. Another rose from the water, leaping from the rear of the boat and wrapping its arms around Shane from behind.

The sudden attack caught him off-balance. He struggled, and the boat lurched. Herbert stayed perfectly rooted in place as the boat tipped nearly ninety degrees and dumped Shane into the murk.

With the ghost's arms tightly around him, Shane sank as he fought against it, thrashing and twisting his body. The light from above swirled as he moved and struggled until he slammed his head back as hard as he could, smacking his skull against the face of his attacker.

The spirit released him, and he turned quickly, scanning the green and brown haze. He saw a flash of movement and though it was not clear what it was, he reached out and took hold.

Shane's hands closed over something, perhaps an arm or a leg. He didn't care what it was, and it didn't matter. He kicked his legs and moved his body, rolling with whatever limb he held and using his weight and leverage to pull and snap it.

The ghost screeched, and Shane kicked again, pushing his body up to the surface. Something scraped against him, scratching his side, and he reached for it, taking hold again. More unseen appendages grasped him from behind and then he rose swiftly, dragging the other ghost with him.

Herbert hoisted Shane from the water, one of his massive hands clutching Shane's collar from behind. Shane had dragged a ghost up with him, its face a mass of bloated flesh so torn that its features were unidentifiable. It had only one arm, having lost the other to Shane below the water.

"Are you okay?" Herbert asked.

"One sec," Shane replied, forcing the drowned ghost back under the water. With his hands on its head, Shane sunk his fingers into the spongy, ghostly flesh. Bits squished between his fingers until he finally got a grip on its skull.

The other ghosts floated nearby, their cries silenced, while Shane applied pressure. The ghost's head was crushed, and water burst in a great splash that would have knocked Shane back under had Herbert not been holding him. Waves crashed against the boat and rolled outward, raising and lowering around the ghosts, who remained untouched by it.

Shane turned, water running down his face, and waited for whichever ghost planned to attack next, but none moved. Instead, a murmur ran through them. He saw faces, among those who still had them, staring in something close to admiration or fear.

"What's happening?" Herbert asked.

"No idea," Shane said, grabbing the edge of the boat. He lifted himself carefully, trying to avoid flipping the small vessel, while the ghosts watched from the water.

"It's called the Custodian," one of the spirits said once Shane was back in the boat.

"What?"

The ghost had drifted near while many of the others kept a distance. It had once been a woman and was missing most of her face. What remained hung from her in soggy gobs of nearly white flesh.

"The ghost you want to find. Long arms and long legs. Eyes like blood. It calls itself the Custodian."

"Why?" Herbert asked.

"I don't know. It's at the school. It stays there. Keeps things there. Victims and trophies. No one goes there anymore."

"No one living?" Shane asked.

"No *one*," the ghost repeated. "It's old. Not as old as Magister, but old."

"And what is the Magister?" Shane asked.

Whispers ran among the spirits assembled around the boat. The ghost that spoke to them drifted closer.

"Magister is Death."

CHAPTER 6

THE SCHOOL

Shane paddled closer to shore while the ghosts from the pond floated with them, trailing behind the vessel. Only the ghost of the woman remained at their side. Only she was willing to keep talking.

"The Custodian has always preyed on children," she told them when Herbert explained why they were hunting it. "Longer than any of us ever knew."

"You don't know who it used to be?" Herbert asked.

"No. Even when Burkitt was still good. Even then, it was already here. Most of us just never knew. It was not as bold back then. Not as greedy."

"Greedy," Shane repeated.

The ghost nodded, her face sagging so much it looked like the flesh would fall away at any moment.

"It has become worse since the town died. Since it had to hunt farther afield. We see it sometimes, out here in the pond."

"Why do you use the word 'it'?" Shane asked.

He resorted to the pronoun himself sometimes when he wasn't sure what he was seeing. Some skeletal spirits had degraded to being "its" when it was no longer possible to tell what sort of person it used to be. But the Custodian was not something like that.

"You'll see," the ghost answered.

Herbert's description of the ghost was of something barely human, but Shane was never sure if that was a result of the passage of time and a memory formed in the heat of panic. Many spirits, especially the more terrifying ones, had inhuman aspects. The rotted flesh, missing parts, horrible wounds. But they were still typically human in appearance.

Shane had supposed that perhaps the Custodian suffered from something called Marfan syndrome, producing elongated limbs and rubbery joints, but it was only a guess. The swamp ghost was right, then. He'd have to see for himself.

The map was wet but still readable, and the ghost showed Shane where the school was as they pulled the boat to the shore near the treeline behind some abandoned Burkitt homes.

"Stay away from Magister's house," the spirit warned. "You will not reach the school if he sees you."

"He's not Death," Shane said. "He's just another ghost. There's no reason to be afraid."

The laughter from the ghost, echoed by the dozens of those that followed, was like a haunting wind at first, something eerie and inhuman.

"You have no idea," the ghost told him. "You cannot know until it's too late."

"Old? Powerful? Deadly? It's a song I've danced to before," Shane assured her.

"Perhaps," the ghost said as Shane got out of the boat and walked the last few steps through the water to dry land. The ghost stayed in the water and watched. "But I have never seen anyone escape him. Many here have tried."

Herbert joined Shane on the shore as the ghosts from the water receded into their murky graves. The school was across the town from the pond, and they needed to cross directly to the far side from where they had landed to get to it.

Shane's curiosity about the Magister and his house was growing. Clearly, the spirit was, if not the center of what had happened in Burkitt, involved in the decay and death of the town. But he was not the ghost they sought, and he would have to sit on the back burner.

If the Magister was old, maybe even the oldest ghost in Burkitt, then perhaps everything could be tied to him. But if the swamp ghosts still feared him, and the hunter ghost had been put on guard by him, then he exerted a strong influence even over the dead. That was something Shane had experienced and knew to be cautious of. A ghost that commanded and intimidated even the dead was dangerous.

Once again, the town of Burkitt reminded Shane of his property on Berkley Street. There were trees, sunlight, and gardens, but it was not a place of life. There was no birdsong, no sign that anything at all lived within the town borders. It was as silent as a grave, save for the faint lapping of water at the swamp's edge.

The swamp ghost had shown them where a path led down to the swamp from the nearby neighborhood, between houses. She said it had once been an access road for fishing when the town was still alive. Now it was overgrown with weeds, brambles, and other plants that tangled on top of one another.

Herbert approached first, drifting through the weeds, and disturbing nothing. Shane took longer, choosing his footing to avoid snags.

The houses on either side of the path were faded with age and lack of care. Years of rain and snow had left everything looking washed out, and the windows were misty with layers of filth. Still, as they passed, Shane saw movement in one house. A face in the window pulled away when he looked at it, something deathly white and nearly devoid of features.

"How many dead do you think are in Burkitt?" Herbert asked, seeing the spirit as well.

"Hard to say," Shane replied. He had guessed the number was high on his first visit, but his journey across the swamp made him rethink things. Before, he suspected maybe a few dozen. Now, he thought the number could be in the hundreds.

"Have you ever seen so many spirits in one place?" the ghost asked.

"Not naturally," Shane replied, "but yeah."

He remembered the hunter referring to the Magister as "kind of a collector". It seemed to Shane that, if there were as many spirits as he suspected, one of two things had happened. Someone had brought them to Burkitt in much the same way Shane carried Herbert's haunted item. Or someone had found a way to cultivate them.

In Shane's experience, it was not possible to make a ghost on purpose. There were ways to increase the likelihood, of course. Many spirits suffered traumatic deaths. Carl and Eloise had died in the Anderson house, trapped and starving in the walls. Their spirits were unsettled and remained. But not every death made a ghost. Not even every murder.

To force a ghost into existence was arguably impossible. But perhaps someone had found a way to play the odds and increase the chances. That someone had to be the Magister, and if he had done such a thing, then he was increasing Burkitt's population of ghosts for a reason. There had to be a purpose behind it, and it had to have been happening for close to a century. Maybe even longer.

Shane's foot snagged on a tangle of brambles. As he pulled away, the weeds parted to reveal a dirt-encrusted skeleton beneath.

"I don't think a lot of people leave this place," Herbert said.

"No, they don't." Shane pulled the thorns loose and continued to the end of the path. They came out onto a street in a neighborhood filled with tall trees and little family homes that were once probably very nice.

The properties were long since overgrown, and a downed tree had crushed one save for the garage. Some had broken windows, and all were dirty and forgotten. Two still had old cars parked in the driveways, now rusted down to little more than frames.

"I don't understand how a whole town can just die," Herbert said, looking up and down the street. Beyond the street's end, past the treetops, the hill on which the Magister's house sat was visible.

"Used to happen when the money ran out. If a town was based on a single industry, it couldn't sustain itself when the industry died. But here? I think it died literally," Shane said.

"The ghosts killed the citizens and only a few have escaped," Herbert said. "People like the ones Lisette had murdered."

"Seems like," Shane agreed. Everything they had seen led him to believe as much.

"But no one did anything. No one sought help, no one reported what was happening here when people died or went missing?"

"That's not what the living do," Shane told him. "If you get attacked by a living assailant, you call the police. If someone drowns in the swamp, it's an accident. If people go hiking and never come back, that's a tragedy. If a sickness claims dozens of lives, that's a reason to try to move on and forget the past. None of them require you to be suspicious of mysterious entities. These ghosts aren't stupid. You saw how they manipulate people."

"It just seems like it could only last for so long," Herbert said. "How many deaths before people get suspicious?"

"Anyone who got suspicious probably ran or died."

"And all of these other people are just forgotten?"

"Some ghosts prey on that," Shane said as he nodded. "They don't always kill. And like you saw, they can work on a person's mind. Make them hear things or see things. Eventually make them do things. It's manipulation. Many people won't realize it's happening because to them, ghosts aren't real. We're all told that all our lives. The voices are not spirits, they're your inner voice. Your conscience. Your mental illness. Whatever way a person can rationalize it. These kinds of ghosts don't care."

"But it's so… wicked," Herbert said. "How could anyone be so evil?"

Shane did not have an answer. The question annoyed him. Herbert was playing naïve. History was full of evil people, it made sense that there would be just as many evil ghosts. More, even, since they were no longer bound by mortal restraints.

If a living person could be a murderous dictator, a serial killer, or a sadist, so could a ghost. The big difference was that the ghost had almost no fear of being caught and no limit on how long it could continue. To

Shane, the question was not how a ghost could be so evil, but how ghosts like Herbert or Carl could retain any of their humanity.

"We shouldn't stay in one place too long," Shane said, looking out over the neighborhood.

More faces were in windows now, some that looked like normal people, and some far more monstrous. The longer they stood still, the more interested the dead became.

They left the path and walked down the center of the street toward the nearest intersection. Even the pavement in Burkitt had suffered the ravages of age. The years of hot summers and cold winters had made it crack, allowing weeds and trees to grow in the crevices. In a few more years, nature would reclaim the roads entirely, and the houses would rot or be overgrown. For now, at least, the roads were the clearest paths to travel.

They reached a rusted stop sign and turned left, heading toward the main street as the ghost had instructed. The skeletal remains of a driver sat slumped in the front of a rusted-out car right at the corner, their ragged clothes hanging from their bones. The ghost was crouched low in the gutted back seat. He peered at them from a pile of leaves and trash, his body covered in slashes like he'd been attacked by a razor. The ghost said nothing, and Herbert and Shane ignored it.

As they approached the main street, Shane slowed their progress and kept close to the houses to avoid being seen, not by ghosts but by the police. Somewhere at the far end of the road they approached was a blockade, but they had no way of knowing if any of the police were still in Burkitt or trying to press into the town. If they were, it would be on the main strip.

Herbert went ahead to scout, confident that he would not be seen by the living. He only reached the sidewalk before he stopped.

"Shane," he shouted back. "You should see this."

Shane moved swiftly, leaving the cover of overgrown hedges and trees and making his way to the road. Herbert waited, standing out in the open until Shane joined him. There was no sign of the living, but there was a state police car.

The vehicle was parked as though it had swerved to avoid something. The driver's door was open, and the driver still had one foot inside the vehicle. The rest of the body was on the road, save for the head, which looked to have been crushed and splattered across the cement as though something had fallen on it from a great height.

"This is recent," Herbert said.

Shane nodded, looking past the car to the street behind it. Nearest to them was the police station that Shane had visited on his previous stop in town. At the far end of the block, behind a wild and full garden, a red brick building covered in windows rose high above the surrounding houses. Burkitt's school awaited.

"Come on," Shane said. "We can't help him."

They left the body and continued.

Somewhere on the street behind them, something laughed.

CHAPTER 7
INTO THE NEST

Shane looked back and saw nothing. The laughter continued, echoing through the abandoned houses. Things moved in the shadows of trees and buildings.

"Go to the police station," Shane instructed, heading toward the building.

"Why there?" Herbert asked.

"I already destroyed the main ghost here. And it has an open back door. We can slip out of sight then keep going."

On his first visit to Burkitt, Shane had looked for some clues about what happened with the carnival and the dead boys. He ran afoul of a dead police officer, but he managed to finish the ghost off. With any luck, the police station was just an empty building now as a result, save for the handful of bodies he'd seen in the back.

The wind worked its way through the tall trees that covered the street and created a nearly impenetrable canopy. Light flickered through the temporary gaps, creating hundreds of dancing shadows. The laughter grew louder.

Shane led Herbert to the police station's door and they headed inside without looking back. The station was small, barely more than a couple of rooms, and the place was a mess. Long before Shane had arrived, someone had gutted much of the building, tossing papers and other items around haphazardly.

The desks and the ancient computers remained, however. It didn't look like someone had looted the station so much as tossed it in search of something specific.

"This way." Shane led Herbert through the front office to the lockup around back.

Shane stopped in the doorway, causing Herbert to pause as well. He had been in the lockup before and seen a couple of cells with bodies locked in them. The place was different now. There were more cells, the room was larger, and there were many more corpses locked in the cells, at least a dozen.

The bodies were old and nearly fully rotted away. They couldn't have been from the family that had just gone missing. But the addition of so many since Shane was last there, and the change to the building layout, was what caused him to freeze.

"We need to be careful here."

"I gathered that already," Herbert replied.

"No," Shane said, shaking his head. "There were half as many cells in this room last time I was here. Half as many corpses."

"They built more cells?" Herbert asked.

"A haunted place can change how it's perceived. It can move rooms or move space to create or hide things. Like what happened at the hospital. Burkitt can do that, too. The whole town is like a haunted house. We can't trust that everything is going to be where we expect it to be all the time."

"So, the map?" Herbert asked.

Shane looked down at it. The police station was marked on the other side of the street and farther up toward the diner. The longer he thought about it, the more sense it made. That was where he had first encountered it. Not here, down the street from a school.

"Useful," Shane answered. "It shows us how things are supposed to be. We might need it to get out of here."

"I don't want to be trapped in this town," Herbert said.

"Neither do I. So let's get moving."

They ignored the new bodies in the back of the police station and headed out the rear into a small parking lot. The school was visible at the end of the road. However things changed in Burkitt, they were not so dramatic as to involve altering the town in the blink of an eye. Or maybe it just didn't want to do that.

They moved swiftly down the street, free from the ghostly laughter and any additional bodies. This part of town suffered the same overgrowth of weeds as everywhere else, but there was an even greater stillness. The closer they got to the school, the fewer shadows danced at the edges of Shane's sight. When they reached the property, there was no sign of any ghosts.

Spirits feared the Custodian. Maybe not all of them, but enough that the property seemed deader than the rest of the town. Burkitt Public School was a red brick building centered below a large clock tower. The clock had no hands; only the stained and aged face remained with dashes in place of numbers.

Below the clock, a wide, paved walkway led to an equally wide staircase and a trio of ancient, worn, wooden double doors that were chained shut. Two floors of windows were mostly obscured with dirt like the rest of the windows in town, but the second floor looked cleaner. Despite that, there was nothing to see behind the glass. Dark rooms and nothing more; no movement or silhouettes. If the Custodian was there, he was not making a scene. He was hidden away.

They stood on the walkway facing the school, and Shane allowed Herbert a moment to take it in.

"This is it," Shane said.

"Yes," Herbert agreed. "If we've been led to the right destination."

"We were," Shane said. It was a gut feeling but one he trusted. Something in the school was keeping other ghosts away. The swamp ghost had no reason to tell them a horrifying thing was in the school if it was something else. He was confident it was in there. Probably watching them.

"I can do this on my own, you know," Herbert said. "I'm the one who came here looking for answers, or closure or—"

"Revenge," Shane interrupted. "You came for revenge, Herbert. You came to face this thing and stop it from killing anyone else ever again. That's what I came for, too."

"But it was never your fight." The ghost was trying to protect Shane, it seemed. Let him off the hook or keep him out of harm's way. It was something he should have known not to do.

"We haven't been friends that long, Herbert, but if we're going to keep being friends, you have to remember who you're talking to."

"I don't want anyone else to die," the ghost explained. Shane smiled and pulled a cigarette out of his pocket, lighting it with his Zippo while he looked from window to window in the school.

"I am not dying in this town, Herbert."

"No one can accuse you of lacking confidence," the ghost replied.

Shane chuckled and started toward the doors. If they found the Custodian and destroyed him, it would go a long way toward finding that missing family. The ghosts that feared the Custodian would think twice about their actions in the wake of his death. They might hold off long enough for Shane and Herbert to find the missing family and get out. That could keep the state police at bay and keep everyone alive. It was a win-win. All they had to do was hunt an inhuman spirit in its lair and take it out.

The two sets of doors to the left were chained and locked tightly, though both the chains and locks were showing their age with corrosion. The doors on the other side had been unlocked at some point. The padlock was missing, and the chain was loose. The door could be pushed enough for someone to slip through.

Herbert went first and signaled Shane the all-clear. Shane looked at the empty street, back the way they had come. Still no sign of ghosts who had come to watch. But the state police cruiser and the dead officer were now missing from the road.

Shane slipped through the door into the dark school. The entrance opened up to a wide lobby lit from above by a skylight that must have been behind the clock tower.

Yellow brick walls still bore posters and signs from when the school was in operation. Some were moldy and impossible to read; others mentioned returning library books, a field trip, and dates to sign up for sports teams.

The halls were littered with detritus. Some was just more paper, even a handful of desks and chairs that had been tossed. Other trash was more out of place, like old beer bottles, a sleeping bag, and evidence of several controlled fires.

Directly beyond the lobby was the school's main office, its sign barely legible under a layer of black mold. Hallways extended to the left and right, both lined with multiple doors, with a third hallway going past the office and deeper into the building.

"Which way?" Herbert asked.

Laughter distracted Shane before he could answer, but it was not the ominous laughter from outside. It was the laughter of children. The spirit of a young boy ran from a doorway and crossed the hall while the ghost of a second gave chase. They were having fun. They weren't frightened or malevolent like the others in town.

Shane headed toward them, trailing smoke as he went, and arrived at the doorway through which they'd run. The two ghost boys were inside a gutted classroom, sharing what looked like a cheese sandwich and giggling quietly.

"I've never seen ghosts eat," Herbert remarked.

Something slammed loudly, and the boys froze, sandwiches forgotten.

"We were just having fun," one of the boys said.

"Oh, that's—" Herbert began.

"Please. We'll go outside," the second boy said, ignoring the big ghost.

"Who are you?" the first boy asked.

"My name is Her—"

The second boy screamed, and his companion joined him. The sandwich fell from their hands, and they raised their arms as something yanked them toward the door, at Shane and Herbert.

The spirits passed between Shane and Herbert and were dragged down the hall, vanishing around a corner. Their screams faded to a ghostly echo and then were silenced.

"What just happened?" Herbert asked.

"They're caught in a memory. They weren't talking to you," Shane said.

Laughter sounded behind them, and Shane turned in time to see the first boy run toward him, past him, and into the room. The second boy followed. They made their way to the corner where they had just been and pulled out. It was the same scene being played out again.

"Is this all they can do?" Herbert wondered.

The two men watched as something came for the boys again, pulled them from the room, and dragged them down the hall until their screams faded to silence. The scene began again with the boys laughing and running into the room a third time.

"Caught in the moment they died," Shane said. "The same events, moments before they were taken. Like a song that gets stuck in your head."

"My God," Herbert whispered. "For how long?"

Shane looked at the boys and pointed at their shaggy hair, the style of their clothes, and their shoes.

"Since the seventies, I think."

The scenario began again, and Shane stepped out of the way to avoid it. He walked back to the room where the boys started, and it was full of children at their desks, while their teacher was having a lecture.

"Who would like to read chapter seven?" the teacher asked. She was a woman in her fifties, in khaki pants and a blouse with a torn-open back that revealed her flayed ribs and spine.

None of the children answered, and Shane exhaled a puff of smoke. The teacher glared at him.

"There is no smoking on school property!" she shouted.

"Not a memory," Shane muttered in response, taking the cigarette from between his lips and holding it down near his waist.

"Do you know where the Custodian is?" Herbert asked.

The teacher's eyes narrowed as she looked from Shane to Herbert.

"In the custodian's office, of course."

"Thank you, ma'am," Herbert said.

The ghost continued glaring until both men had left the room. The door slammed shut in their wake, but the two boys continued to run through it in their repeated loop.

"I don't understand what's happening in here," Herbert said.

"Just… habit, I suppose," Shane explained. "Victims of the Custodian playing out bits of their lives."

"But she talked to us," the ghost said. "It's not a memory; it's real-time."

"With rules, I would guess," Shane told him. "Maybe the Custodian wants things to stay the same in the school as much as possible. He's created a place that doesn't change. That isn't allowed to change."

"A place his victims can't escape," Herbert said as though just realizing it. "He's keeping them all here, so he doesn't have to stop watching them suffer. He can relive their torment again and again."

"Possibly," Shane said.

He could see the turmoil on the big ghost's face.

"I know you're not used to this, so don't let your guard down. You don't ever want to assume a ghost is going to be like your best friend, your mom, whoever. A dead body rots, and a soul can, too. They get twisted and dark. Any nightmare you can imagine, they can be worse. Keep that in mind."

"How do you live in this world?"

There was real fear in Herbert's voice. Shane returned the cigarette to his lips and shrugged.

"It's the only world I got."

He headed down the hall in the direction the ghosts of the two boys had been dragged. If they were reliving their abduction by the Custodian, then they were showing Shane where to go.

The hall branched out, and the ghosts were dragged to the right. As the scenario played out again, Shane watched the boys get pulled down the dark corridor to some stairs and then down below. The light from the lobby skylight didn't reach any of it, and they were left in total darkness.

"Keep your eyes open," Shane said, using his lighter to illuminate the stairs as they approached. The stairway led to a landing, turned, and then went further down to a level they could not see from their vantage point.

"Are you sure we shouldn't search up here first?" Herbert asked.

Shane nodded and took the first step.

Those boys were dragged into the dark, so into the dark was where they needed to go.

CHAPTER 8

THE BASEMENT

The sound of whispers filled every shadow in the school basement. They were too muffled to make out, but they were the voices of children. As soon as one stopped, another began in a different dark corner.

More trash was piled in the basement. In places, it looked like someone had built barriers out of chairs and desks, some covering half of the hall and others knocked aside as though whatever they were meant to hold back had pushed through the blockade.

The smell in the basement was not unfamiliar. It was the smell of the outside of a slaughterhouse. Not strong but threatening to unleash something if you get too close.

In the distance, a scream pierced the darkness and echoed along the halls, silencing the whispers. The flame on Shane's lighter flickered as the scream was cut off, a wet crunch ending it abruptly.

A shadow ran down the hall, not a ghost with any recognizable shape, just darkness moving swiftly. It rushed past Shane and Herbert, and the sound of panicked breathing followed it.

"Please," one of the whispers said.

"Please," another joined in.

"Please."

"Please!"

"PLEASE!"

A desperate chorus of begging and pleading echoed all around them. There were no more demands, just that one word, again and again, the tone and inflection and voice changing with every utterance. The sound was pure panic and dread each time it was spoken.

The hallways in the basement were like a maze. Doors were unlabeled and most were locked. Some were caked in sludge that could have once been something living, though Shane was in no rush to get close enough to test.

The whispers were nearly ceaseless, and the screams came and went, but no ghosts manifested where Shane could see them. Even Herbert could see nothing in the darkness.

The cold was bitter, and it seeped into Shane's exposed flesh. They walked the halls, pushing past desks and trash, searching open rooms for any sign of the spirit they sought.

"There's something up here," Shane observed as they neared the end of one hall. The space opened into some kind of foyer before a set of large double doors.

"Cafeteria," Herbert said, reading the sign on the wall. He was answered by a scream from the other side of the door and more rushing shadows fleeing down the hall the way they had come.

Herbert headed inside first, passing through the wall to scout for danger. Shane waited for him to return and as the seconds ticked by, he felt the cold air closing in around him more deeply. The whispers seemed more focused, and shapes danced at the edge of the flickering flame in his hand.

Minutes passed, and Shane approached the double doors.

"Herbert," he said, his hand resting on the handle. The ghost did not reply.

Shane pushed the door in, and a rush of thick, rancid air escaped the room. Shane felt his stomach knot involuntarily, and the cigarette dropped from his mouth as his body tensed. He was forced to steady himself just to keep from vomiting.

The smell was overwhelming, but he pushed it from his mind. It was the stench of mass death, and things rotten and damp. He retrieved the cigarette from the floor and pinched it out before entering the cafeteria.

"Jesus…" was all Herbert said.

There were lights in the cafeteria, impossible lights set into the walls, powered by some kind of spirit energy. A perverse whim of the Custodian, perhaps, to prevent darkness from hiding his crimes.

The room was ransacked, destroyed even, with flipped tables and piled chairs. But there were dozens of bodies in the mayhem. Banners of flesh hung from the stacked chairs like flags. Heads filled stock pots in the kitchen, warming trays overflowed with bile and limbs. Blood and gore were splattered across walls from floor to ceiling, now rotted black with age.

Children, Shane thought. The bodies were mostly children. Those that could still be recognized as bodies. The rest was like something run through a meat grinder. The dim wall sconces bathed it all in a sickly yellow light. No corner was hidden, no atrocity kept out of sight.

Herbert turned, pushed past Shane, and left the room without a word. Shane let him go. There was no reason to stay there. This was not the Custodian's lair. It was his trophy room.

Shane followed Herbert, the door falling shut behind him. As it clicked, the sound reverberated down the halls. More yellow sconces flickered to light, and the basement lit up in all directions. There was no doubt now that the Custodian knew they were coming.

There were ghosts now. They cowered in the corners, in the places that were dark before. They hid under the upturned desks and chairs, huddled together like animals in a storm.

Some of the spirits were still identifiable as children. Some were remnants of what had been done to them, missing eyes, jaws, even faces. A few ran when Shane laid eyes on them, realizing that the cloak of darkness had been pulled away. Others were just frozen in place. Some snarled and hunkered down like wild animals that might strike at any moment. They had lost their lives and their humanity as part of the

Custodian's prison.

Shane wondered how long the Custodian had worked in the school. How long had he tortured and killed while people still lived in Burkitt? To achieve such numbers would have taken years. Years and years of parents losing children and… what? Herbert was not wrong to think that Burkitt's evil was unfathomable. Something worse than Shane had ever encountered was happening there, but he could not explain it.

"Where is the Custodian?" Shane asked the children.

The ghosts whispered, fast and panicky, none speaking directly to Shane. Those he approached shrank into the walls and vanished. He was forced to stand and wait, straining to make out what they were saying.

Much of the chatter was impossible to understand. The word "Custodian" was repeated, but so was "Magister". Some whispered warnings, some begged to leave.

"Where is he?" Shane asked again.

The ghosts would not answer clearly. Shane approached several more, but they all pulled away. The yellow lights flickered, and the whispering became louder but less clear.

Shane shook his head and started down the next hall, with Herbert behind him. They would get no answers from the spirits, and Shane did not want to waste any more time.

Bathed in the yellow light, they passed room after room. Some were cluttered, and some held ghosts, but none were what they were looking for. He walked faster, his frustration growing, until he saw a white hand pulling the door near the end of the hall shut.

Shane ran, the chorus of whispers trailing behind as he reached the door and threw it open, Herbert forgotten in the hall.

Sunlight caused him to squint and raise his hand. He was no longer in the basement. It was brightly lit, with windows showing sunshine and trees in the yard. A cushioned table was against the far wall, alongside a cabinet full of gauze, bandages, and more. The school nurse, her back to Shane, was doing paperwork at the desk in front of him.

"Where is the Custodian?" he asked.

The nurse closed the folder she was working on and stood. She wore an old-school nurse's uniform with a small, white hat atop a head of honey-colored hair held up in a bun, flat shoes, and an ankle-length white dress.

The nurse turned, and her face was streaked with blood. Her eyes had been cut from her head at some point, the act performed with a tool that left the area ragged and messy.

Her jaw was offset, broken from the look of it, and hung open exposing the stump of a missing tongue. She hissed, the action causing drops of dark blood to spray from her mouth.

Shane's back hit the door, slamming it shut. The nurse attacked with her teeth bared, trying to bite his face as she ran to him with full force. Her body pressed against his and her teeth gnashed, nearly sinking into his cheek.

He head-butted the ghost, smashing her nose with his forehead and giving himself enough space to push her back across the room and steady himself. The space in which they fought was small, and it made maneuvering difficult. The nurse's random attacks made it hard to predict and counter her movements.

They wrestled awkwardly, Shane on the defensive and just trying to keep the ghost away from him long enough to come up with a counter, but she was like an attack dog, rushing and gnashing her teeth over and over. Even when he caught her left arm and broke it at the elbow, she didn't pause.

The door opened, and Herbert appeared. Shane fell back as the nurse lunged again and he landed in the hallway. The nurse spread her jaws and leaned in, ready to snap at his throat. Herbert grabbed her by the hair and yanked her upward.

The distraction was all the opportunity Shane needed. He reached up and took the ghost's head in his hands just as Herbert lost his grip, the hair pulling away and revealing a bloody skull in its wake.

She fell forward again but Shane held on to her this time, gripping her far enough away that she could not reach him with her teeth.

"Kill me," the nurse whispered as she brought her face close to his, her empty eyes bleeding onto his face. For a moment, he thought he had not heard her correctly, or that it was the whispers of the other spirits.

"Kill me. End it."

The words were pleading and there was desperation in the expression on her face. Shane gripped her head tightly, pushing up and away from his body. She thrashed in his grip, her one good hand clawing at his wrists. Her skull snapped, and for an instant, she stopped fighting. A smile crossed her lips and then her skull crumbled in Shane's hands.

He was blown backward as the force of the spirit's destruction slammed down on them like a ton of bricks, knocking the air from his lungs and causing him to roll over and cough.

The illusion of the nurse's office was gone. The sunlight vanished, replaced with the dank, yellow lights and the entrance to a dark passageway beyond the door.

Herbert was first to his feet while Shane took a moment longer. The ghosts were gone, all of them silent and missing even from their hiding places. Shane sat up and looked into the room he'd uncovered. A tiled hallway extended into the shadows; a bank of lockers was on his left, and shelves of cleaning supplies filled the space to the right. It looked like the sort of room a custodian might use.

"Shane, I think this is the place," Herbert whispered as Shane got back to his feet.

"Don't. Keep. Me. Waiting," a staccato voice replied from the depths of the shadows. It was deep but off somehow, like someone faking an accent.

Waiting. Waiting. Waiting.

The word echoed, distorted and inhuman, repeated by the whispering ghosts as a soft murmur that filled the dark space once more.

"What can you see?" Shane asked. Herbert shook his head.

"I can't see into that darkness."

The Custodian was happy to stay hidden and was going out of his way to do so. It didn't matter to Shane. They would find him.

Shane headed into the room and took a broom from the cleaning supplies, breaking the handle in half over his knee.

"What are you doing?" Herbert asked.

"Making things brighter," Shane said. He grabbed a cleaning rag from a shelf, wrapped it with a heavy knot around one end, and then soaked it with some lemon-scented furniture polish that was stored above various detergents and floor cleaners.

They returned to the impenetrably dark hallway. The ghost voices still whispered, their words a muddled and unintelligible cacophony of fear and panic.

Shane pulled out his Zippo and flicked the wheel, igniting a flame. He brought the broomstick close, and the fumes from the rag ignited in a bright, fiery flash. The light filled the space and gave Shane a quick glimpse of a small, disheveled room with a cot and some shelves among a tangle of pipes and cables coming out of the walls.

The fire took hold of the torch. Shane took a cigarette from his pack and placed it between his lips, bringing the Zippo close to light it before tucking it back into his pocket.

"You ready?" he asked.

Herbert nodded but did not say anything.

They headed down the hall together.

CHAPTER 9
THE CUSTODIAN

The hallway to the Custodian's room was barely six steps long, and they were soon in what looked like a cramped general utility room that someone had converted into a makeshift apartment long ago. Next to the cot was a small office fridge, and a dusty hotplate sat on a table next to that. There were old magazines, wrinkled with age and dampness, as well as piles of clothes, bottles, and food wrappers. It looked like the sort of place squatters had claimed in secret.

The light of the torch flickered and struggled, the black smoke it produced rising in thick tendrils to the ceiling. Shane swept it from one side of the room to the other. The walls were laced with large and small pipes, the gas and water supply for the school running through the space, it seemed.

"There." Herbert pointed to the corner.

Beyond the thick, cast-iron plumbing stack, in the corner opposite the cot, a tall, slender, milky-white figure was pressed into the shadows. Shane could only see part of the spirit, just an arm, a leg, and part of the face, but Herbert's description had failed to do it justice.

The Custodian's flesh looked like that of an albino lizard, glossy smooth and devoid of any pigment. The features were not like those of a fully formed human. The nostrils did not curve before the nose joined the cheeks, and the lips were barely there. Even the eyes, as red as blood, were the opposite of sunken. They seemed almost even with the smooth flesh of its face, with little to distinguish the lids.

The Custodian was hairless. Its arms and legs were as Herbert had described, almost impossibly long and terribly thin. Even the fingers on the one hand Shane could see were too long. Its appearance was not impossible, just not right. Like a dozen bizarre events had to have occurred to leave it in such a state.

Shane had seen many ghosts that defied reason. Ghosts that had died such horrid deaths that their spirits were little more than walking nightmares. He could only imagine the suffering they had gone through to make them what they were. But he could not imagine what had happened to the Custodian. He had no way to explain it. Perhaps some extremely unfortunate genetic condition; something like what had happened to Dash to make him into the Alligator Boy at the carnival.

"Is that what made you target him?" Shane asked.

The Custodian's lipless mouth smiled, revealing teeth that were too small.

"What does that mean?" Herbert asked.

"Dash. The Alligator Boy. He was different. He looked different. That's what drew him out. Made him leave the confines of Burkitt to where the carnival was set up."

"Different. Ha. Ha. Ha," the Custodian said. His voice still sounded far away and strained, even this close.

"But why let the people kill him? Why kill him if they were so alike?" Herbert asked, more of the ghost than of Shane.

"It hated him," Shane replied before turning to the Custodian. "You hated him. And those people. Didn't you?"

He knew none of this for sure. But seeing the Custodian now, seeing its face and the way it reacted to his words, he felt he was right. The Custodian didn't kill Dash. It killed the boys from Burkitt. And then it made the people of Burkitt kill Dash. It riled them up and made them hate the freak. And it knew that would work because the Custodian had already gone through it once.

"Is that how you died? Someone in town turned on you? Found out what you were like and killed you?"

Shane had no doubt it was not innocent. Back when it was alive, when it was a man of some kind, he'd probably killed a child. Maybe more than one. And when the citizens of Burkitt found out, they ended it their way. They killed the Custodian, the town freak, and freed him to become an even bigger monster.

"So. Smart," the Custodian whispered. Its red eyes darted to Herbert, and the unsettling smile grew wider. "Remember. You. I remember."

"I remember you, too," Herbert said coldly.

Shane's torch continued to flicker, the fuel and the rag having been nearly used up. The Custodian licked its lips.

"Dark. Soon," it said. "Bye-bye. Bye-bye, light."

It giggled in an eerie way as Shane drew back his hand and threw the torch into the corner. He ran toward the spirit and the last, flickering flames. The Custodian's jaw fell open as it let loose a deep, uproarious laugh and latched onto the walls, climbing like an insect to the ceiling.

Shane took hold of one long, thin leg by the ankle and pulled, dragging the ghost from the ceiling as the torch continued to flicker. Shane kept his grip on its leg.

They fell to the ground together and Shane brought an elbow down as hard as he could into whatever was close. The Custodian howled as its leg snapped below the knee. The body shuddered and writhed in Shane's grip. Something slashed him across the face, and he cursed as he felt blood flow from a wound above his eyes.

He began punching, slamming fists into anything he could land on. Ghostly flesh buckled and pulsed, and the spirit let out grunts and growls as it struggled to free itself.

The ghost caught Shane's fist mid-punch, and he felt one of his fingers bend back against his hand. The bone broke quickly, and he bit off a scream as pain shot up his arm.

The sound of liquid splashing preceded a small explosion, and Shane was forced to cover his eyes as a ball of flame filled the space. The Custodian was above him sideways, equally surprised by the fire. The bottle of floor polish Shane had used to make the torch was in the middle of the blaze, born from the smoldering scraps of his improvised torch.

Herbert bellowed, running from the supply shelf where he'd retrieved the bottle. His incredible bulk looked like a truck speeding down a freeway as it came toward them.

Shane rolled aside just as Herbert lunged, slamming into the Custodian like a bear pouncing on prey. The impact sent them across the room and into the fire. Herbert held the spirit down in the flames and slammed its pale, hairless head against the tile floor again and again.

The Custodian squealed and struggled like a wild animal, but Herbert's size and ferocity were beyond his powers. The big ghost pulled a pale arm off at the shoulder like removing the wing from a fly, his other hand clasped over the Custodian's face as he continued to smash it on the floor.

"Why did you kill them?" Herbert demanded, his voice louder and angrier than Shane had heard before.

"Love. Them. Hate. Them," the Custodian warbled, its voice strained and panicked.

"WHY DID YOU KILL HIM?"

The temperature of the room dropped drastically, and Shane gasped from the rush like he had been plunged into a frozen river. Herbert's rage was fully unleashed now. The fire paled to a sickly, nearly white flame, and he took the Custodian's other arm in his hands, forcing it up straight. He said nothing before opening his mouth and biting down on the soft, white wrist. The Custodian shrieked but Herbert did not stop, biting off the ghost's hand and spitting it into the flames.

"Not. Me! Not. Bad! Magister's rule. Magister's permission!" the Custodian blathered, its body bucking and wriggling beneath Herbert's enormity.

Shane could not help the other ghost while he was immersed in flames and could only watch from close by. Herbert's rage was powerful, and he did not want to interfere until he had to.

"Tell me!" Herbert shouted, slamming a fist into the Custodian's face. "Tell me!"

"Magister's rule! Magister. Let. Me. Rule here. My home. My Kingdom!" the ghost stammered around squeals and moans as Herbert continued his beating.

"Who is the Magister?" Shane asked.

Herbert seemed shocked by the question, as though he had been lost in his rage and forgot Shane was even there. He stopped beating the Custodian, and the pale ghost's head lolled to one side, its jaw broken. It fixed red eyes on Shane and giggled again.

"Magister of all. Magister of everything."

"He runs the town; I get it. But why? Who was he?"

The giggling continued as the fire began to burn itself out.

"Magister of everything. Everything!"

Shane shook his head while the Custodian continued to laugh. He only had one working leg now, a broken jaw, and a missing hand, and still, he laughed.

"He's useless," Shane said.

They would get no answers to satisfy Herbert's rage, or even explain why Burkitt was the way it was. The Custodian was not an integral part of that nightmare. It was just a monster, a mindless beast.

Herbert's anger seemed to drain away like water through cracks in the floor. The chill in the room lessened. He stared down at the thing beneath him with disappointment and frustration.

"You can't even understand."

The Custodian laughed.

"Help me!"

The voice came from back the way they had come. Shane looked at Herbert, and it was clear the ghost was having the same thought. The cry for help was from a child, not a ghost. Something in the tone of the voice was not like the ghost children had been.

"Who is that?" Shane demanded, staring at their captive.

Herbert let up on the Custodian, but even in its wounded state, the ghost was ready to move. It scrambled, kicking with its broken leg, and using its stump arm to try to pull itself away from its attackers.

"Help me!" the voice cried out again. The Custodian laughed and fixed wild, red eyes on Shane.

"Will. Eat," it hissed. Herbert caught it by its one good leg before it could scramble farther.

Now that the fire was almost out, Shane could reach it again. The madness of the Custodian, the evil within, was not something that could be negotiated with. It was a rabid animal, and there was only one choice left.

Herbert held the ghost while Shane pushed its head down into the tile. It switched between screaming and laughing as the pale, thin body writhed like an unearthed worm. It spouted gibberish; words and phrases that made no sense. Somehow, the pathetic display made Shane even angrier. He grasped the back of its smooth head and squeezed as hard as he could.

The Custodian burst with a hollow, wet sound. Herbert tumbled back into the flames and Shane was knocked back to the hallway near the supply room. His broken finger throbbed, and he tore a strip from his shirt as he sat up, wrapping it around the broken finger to secure it before he stood up again.

"Are you okay?" Herbert approached him and gestured at his face. Shane wiped his forehead, and his hand came away saturated in blood. The cut was deep but not life-threatening. It was just bleeding a lot.

"I'll be fine." Shane turned to look back into the rest of the basement. "That call for help was from someone alive—"

"The missing family." Herbert's eyes widened.

Shane got to his feet and headed into the cluttered darkness.

CHAPTER 10
THE BOY

"You should yell," Herbert suggested.

"No," Shane said.

"They'll hear you."

"So will everything else in this town," he pointed out.

"Then how will we find them?"

Shane held up his lighter, looking around in the moving light. The other ghosts had returned, the children who fled when the Custodian appeared.

"Is there someone alive here?" Shane asked. No one answered.

"He's gone now. You don't have to be afraid," Herbert told them. "The Custodian is gone."

The ghosts whispered loudly, frantically. The words were lost but soon they slipped into shadows, just a few at first, then more.

"He's dead," someone said.

"He's dead!"

"Dead!"

"Dead!"

"Dead!"

More spirits joined the chorus. Shadows darted every which way. Others came out full, visible now as the children they once were. They ran, some upstairs, and some down the halls. The whispers were soon replaced with yells and whoops. Even laughter.

Herbert smiled, listening to the medley of voices get louder. Dozens of ghosts ran past them, through walls and clutter, rousing more and more.

Shane lost count of them all, but like the swamp outside of town, it was easy to see there were many more than he'd guessed. The Custodian had been prolific.

Something banged loudly, but the sound came from above.

"Help!" the voice called again.

"Upstairs," Herbert confirmed. "I'll go find it."

"I'll be right behind you," Shane said.

The ghost rose through the floor while Shane made his way to the stairs. Things were frantic in the school as spirits sprinted around, laughing, and shouting. It was like the last day of school before summer; the children were thrilled to finally be free.

They were all still trapped, of course. Whatever rooted them there was still there, but they were no longer going to be tormented, at least not by the Custodian. The Magister was another matter.

If the Custodian's rantings were to be believed, then the Magister let the Custodian have the school and the children to placate it. Like a lord given land by its king. But how had the Magister become king? What could place it above something like the Custodian and give it control?

Shane reached the main floor. Classroom doors were open up and down the halls, and sunlight now filled the space. The ghosts' laughter echoed all around him.

There was no sign of Herbert. Shane was hopeful that the big ghost could handle his emotions regarding the Custodian and what had happened. He had unleashed a serious dose of hate and anger, but only for a moment. And now that the Custodian was destroyed, there was no one else for Herbert to hold accountable for what had happened all those years ago. Everyone involved was gone.

It might not have been the closure the ghost wanted. The Custodian would never have provided a rational or acceptable reason for what it did. But it was something, at least. No one else would die because of the Custodian. No one else would fall victim to the nightmare it had created.

Not anymore.

Shane rounded a corner as Herbert appeared from a classroom halfway down the hall.

"Anything?" Shane yelled.

"No," Herbert answered, just as banging from the nearby lockers drowned his voice.

"Hey! I'm in here!"

The sound came from inside of one of the army green lockers set into the wall. Shane approached it quickly and Herbert joined him as he lifted the latch on a rusty locker missing the number plate to identify it.

A boy spilled out onto the floor and scrambled across the hall in search of somewhere to hide. He rolled onto his back and looked up at Shane and Herbert with terror.

"Please, don't hurt me," he begged, holding up his hands and turning away with his eyes scrunched shut.

"It's good. You're fine, kid," Shane assured him.

"Shane," Herbert said softly. "Wipe your face."

"What?"

Shane touched his face again. Blood was still running from the scratch on his forehead. He used his sleeve to wipe across his eyes and cheeks.

"That blood's mine," Shane said, crouching in front of the child. "Got a cut. Not going to hurt you, I promise."

The boy opened his eyes tentatively, still holding out his hands and taking in deep, panicked breaths. He was covered in dirt and rust from the locker. His face bore several bruises and scrapes, as did his hands.

"Are you okay?" Herbert asked.

"Everyone's missing," the boy blurted out. "The mechanic took my dad, and my mom and Hailey were getting food, and I never saw them again. You gotta help them!"

"We will. If we can," Herbert said. "But are you okay?"

The boy stared at Herbert, lips trembling, and eyes damp with tears.

Shane wondered if he knew Herbert was a ghost, or if he'd even seen a ghost before that day. He could certainly see them now.

"Are you guys cops?"

"No," Shane said. "This isn't a cop thing, is it?"

The boy's mouth worked for a moment as though he was trying to say something, then he shook his head.

"They're not people. The mechanic, he wasn't… and the thing that took me here. He's not real."

"He was," Shane said. "But he's gone now."

"He'll come back. He told me he'd come back," the boy whispered.

"He won't anymore," Herbert said. "We made sure."

The boy reached out quickly and grabbed Shane's hand.

"You're real," he said.

He scrambled forward and threw himself at Shane, wrapping his arms around him tightly. Shane accepted the gesture awkwardly and looked at Herbert.

"C'mon," Herbert whispered, miming a hug. Shane put one arm tentatively around the boy.

"Real as it gets, see?" Shane said. "What's your name, kid?"

"Jason." The boy buried his face in Shane's chest.

"Okay, Jason. We're going to get you out of here, see if we can find the rest of your family. Your dad, mom, and sister, right?"

"Yes, sir," Jason said, pulling away.

"Good, okay. My name is Shane, and my friend here is Herbert." Shane pulled his arm away and got to his feet, forcing the boy to do the same.

"Is my family still alive?" Jason asked shakily. Shane wiped his face again and glanced at Herbert.

"You want me to be honest?"

The boy bit back a sob and nodded while Herbert frowned.

"Truth is, I don't know. But you're alive, so there's a chance. Do you

76

know what happened here? Do you understand what took you?"

"Some kind of monster."

"Sort of. It was a ghost. This town is full of ghosts," Shane told him. "You're going to need to be able to handle that for a while. Until we can get out of here."

"My mom always said ghosts aren't real," Jason said. The laughter of the children who were now free of the Custodian was still all around them. Shane shrugged.

"Well, yeah, moms will say that. They'll tell you Santa Claus is real, too."

"Why didn't they get you?" the boy asked.

"They tried," Shane said, showing off his broken finger as he gestured to the cut on his face. "But I can handle them."

"You can fight ghosts?"

"Yep," Shane said. "And Herbert here is a ghost, so you need to not freak out when you see him do ghost stuff, or this is going to be a lot harder than it needs to be."

Jason took a step back, eyes now locked on Herbert.

The big man sighed. "You didn't need to tell him that."

"I don't work with a lot of kids," Shane said. "I don't want him losing his mind if you walk through a wall."

Shane turned back to Jason.

"Look, he's a good ghost. I wouldn't work with him if he wasn't. Don't worry."

"A... good ghost?" the boy whispered. Herbert smiled reassuringly.

"There are more out there than you'd think," Shane said.

"Why don't we get out of the school?" Herbert suggested. "Out into the light and fresh air?"

"Yeah. Are you ready to go?" Shane asked the boy.

"Yes, please," he replied, still watching Herbert warily.

They led the boy down the halls and back to the front entrance of the building. The doors that were previously chained had been torn from their hinges, and now, a breeze from outside blew in. Shane could see ghosts on the front lawn of the school and up and down the streets, running to wherever they felt they needed to go.

He didn't know how the other ghosts in town would react to the Custodian's prisoners being free, and he wasn't sure if it mattered. The Magister was going to be the problem.

"That's where it got us," the boy said, pointing into the distance. Beyond the trees and houses was the hill that Shane and Herbert had been told to avoid. The Magister's house.

"What happened?" Shane asked. They stood on the steps in a patch of warm sun, looking at the building in the distance.

"Our car broke down at this tree in the middle of the road. The people in town were all friendly, and they told us to go there. Mom and Hailey went to the diner, and me and Dad went there to see the mechanic. He was old and weird, and then something pulled us into the basement," Jason explained.

"And then?"

"Then I was here. And the monster said he'd be back. And then you came."

"You didn't see what happened to your father?" Herbert asked.

"No," the boy answered. "Can you save him like you saved me?"

"We'll try," Shane said, mostly to himself.

The Magister was the power in Burkitt, and he did not want to face him without a plan or any idea of what he was getting into. Nothing that so many ghosts feared was going to be an easy fight.

They needed time and strategy. Maybe some kind of intel if there was any to gather.

"And your mom and sister were up that way?" Shane asked, pointing in the opposite direction to a place lost in the trees.

"I think so," the boy answered. "There was a diner right next to the tree."

Shane remembered the tree in the road from his first visit. There was no diner at that time, though. Not a functional one. The ghosts had rolled out the red carpet for Jason's family, making it look like a real, living town.

"We're going to look for your mom and sister first," Shane said. "We can get a better idea of what we're dealing with back that way, too. Then, we'll find a way to save your dad if we can."

"You gotta save him. Please," Jason pleaded.

"We'll do our best," Herbert assured the boy. "Just remember to stay close and let us know if you see anything."

"Well, you're going to see lots of things," Shane pointed out. "Just watch for anything coming after us, I guess."

They headed the rest of the way down the steps and up the road to the main street in town. There were no more laughing ghosts or anything that Shane could see. To the left, far up the street, he made out the tree the boy spoke of.

"Let's go see what we can find."

CHAPTER 11

THE JUNKYARD

There were no looming spirits as they approached the tree in the center of the road. Where before there had been dozens in the shadows and watching from windows, now there was nothing. Either the destruction of the Custodian or word from the Magister had sent them into hiding.

"None of it was like this before," Jason said as they walked. "Everything looked new and clean, and there were people everywhere."

The houses were all ramshackle and falling apart, as they had been when Herbert and Shane came in off the swamp. The ghosts had shown a thriving town to Jason's family, a trick to lure them toward the Magister's house. Now there was no need to maintain the deception.

"Ghosts can do that sometimes," Shane said. "Show you things that aren't real. Helps confuse you, trick you into doing something you shouldn't."

"Can you do that?" Jason asked Herbert.

They were half a block from the tree and there was still no sign of life or death.

"Illusions, you mean?" the ghost asked.

"Yeah. Can you make people see stuff?"

"Oh. I've never tried," Herbert answered.

"Not something every ghost can do," Shane added. "Usually, it takes stronger ones. Ones that have been around a while and want to trick people."

"So not good ones?" the boy said.

"The good ones can do it too. I know a ghost who can change how he looks. Make himself look older than he was when he died. And he's one of the good ones. Usually, the bad ones do it to scare or even hurt people"

They approached the tree, and Shane slowed his pace. The boy had said the car died at the tree, but there was nothing on the street.

"Mom!" Jason yelled. The child ran to a building on the far side of the street. Long ago, it had been a diner, but most of the windows were broken now and the interior was almost completely gutted. Nothing was there.

"Mom!"

"Hold on a moment," Herbert said, joining the boy. "Let me look first."

He passed Jason and drifted through the exterior wall, moving swiftly through the broken-down dining room.

"What kind of car were you driving?" Shane asked, distracting the boy while Herbert searched.

"An SUV." Jason looked at the street and then farther up toward the edge of town. There was no vehicle.

"It's gone. What if they left?" he said, looking up at Shane.

"Your family?" he asked. The boy nodded, his eyes threatening to well up again.

"I don't think so," Shane said. "They wouldn't leave you. Your car probably got moved."

Shane pulled out the map and unfolded it. The diner was not far from the junkyard Herbert had pointed out before. It was as good a place as any to hide a car. The only vehicles in town were rusted-out antiques except for the state police car they'd seen, which had vanished like the family's SUV. They'd want to keep the new ones out of sight.

"No one is here," Herbert said, returning from the diner. "I'm sorry."

"Where did they go?" Jason asked.

Shane was not sure how to answer. There was a good chance they were already dead, but the boy didn't need to know that. Of course, he had assumed the same about Jason, and yet he was alive. There was simply no way to know where they were, or how they were.

"This isn't a big town, kid. We'll keep looking."

"But where?" The boy was growing frantic.

Shane turned the map around, showing it to Herbert and the boy.

"Johnny's Scrapyard," he said.

A gust of wind raced up the street at his words, rustling the map and threatening to pull it from his hands. The sound of a faint, low groan came with it. Shane grunted and peered back toward the house on the hill that he had been warned against approaching. The place where the boy and his father were taken. He was sure it was the central hub of Burkitt.

There was nothing to see. No spirits crept in the shadows. No faces were hidden in murky windows. The ghosts were going to let him spin his wheels for a while, and then perhaps try something later when they felt he'd let his guard down.

Shane turned and looked back in the other direction. The road out of Burkitt was lonely and bare. It rose up a hill through the woods, and the angle of the hill meant there was little to see.

Somewhere in the distance was the police blockade. He and Herbert had seen several cars there, the strength of the force present. The fact that they were still waiting didn't instill much confidence in Shane. They were planning something, and his window to find the boy's family was shrinking.

"Let's go while we still have light," Shane said, not wanting to worry the boy with the police issue. He turned his back on the diner and followed the map's directions to a nearby side street. The boy followed at his side with Herbert a step behind, keeping watch at their rear.

"Where did all the people go?" Jason asked as they walked.

"No one lives here," Shane answered. "Not anymore."

The road had no sidewalk and was bordered on each side by tiny homes, most of them covered by aluminum siding with overgrown shrubs planted in front of tiny porches. It could have been any neighborhood in any town in America during a week when the landscapers were on strike.

"There were a whole bunch of people when we got here," Jason explained.

"Again, just a trick," Shane told him.

"Like hypnosis?"

"Sort of," Shane replied. There was no quick way to explain ghost illusions. Especially on the streets of a ghost town. He didn't add anything else as they kept walking.

Still, nothing moved in the windows. The ghosts were not being coy here; they had gone into hiding. Something else was going on that Shane was not fully aware of. But he wasn't going to look a gift horse in the mouth, either. If they were letting him wander the town without resistance, so be it.

"Is this too easy?" Herbert asked as they crossed to the next block and encountered more of the same.

"It is," Shane answered simply.

"What does that mean?" Jason asked them. Shane glanced at Herbert, who looked like he regretted mentioning it.

"Just thinking out loud," the ghost said.

"What does *that* mean?" the boy asked again.

"Means it's very strange that no one is around right now," Shane said.

"But you said no one lives here."

Shane sighed. At least Eloise had been alive long enough to talk like an adult more often than not, even if she fell into some child-like behavior now and then. He was not keen on watching children.

"Everyone here is dead, kid," Shane told him.

"What?" the boy asked, stopping on the street.

Shane sighed again and turned to face him, just as Herbert knelt at the boy's side.

"The people of this town, he means," Herbert explained. "They're ghosts. Like the one who took you, they're all... restless spirits. And some of them are dangerous, like you saw. So, we're a little nervous that they're all missing. But you don't need to worry, because that also means none of them can hurt you anymore, okay?"

"But my mom and dad. And Hailey," Jason whimpered. Herbert nodded.

"I know. It's scary. I lost some of my family, too. The same ghost who hurt you, hurt a boy I loved very much, a long time ago."

"You used to live here?"

"No. We were just visiting. Like you and your family. And that ghost found us and did what he did, and that's why I came back here with Shane. To make sure he could never do that again. And now, he never will. And if we stopped him, we can stop anything else this town has."

"So, they're going to be okay? My family?"

Shane waited for Herbert to make the impossible promise the boy was asking him to make. They didn't know if the family was okay. Herbert knew that. The boy probably knew it, too. But he wanted someone to tell him he was wrong.

"How old are you, Jason?" Herbert asked.

"Twelve," the boy replied. The ghost nodded.

"Twelve. You're not a little kid then, are you? You're old enough to know when things are bad, right?"

Jason fought to hold back tears, but he nodded.

"I don't know where your family is. I don't know if they're okay. I'm like you; this is all new to me. But we're doing it together, okay? I promise to stick with you until we know what happened, alright? And I trust my friend Shane. He's the toughest guy I ever met, and I once knew the World's Strongest Man. But Shane's tougher than him. We're going to do everything we can to find your family, okay?"

"Okay," the boy replied softly, sniffing.

He held back his tears, though it was very close. Shane pulled a cigarette from his pack and gave Herbert a quick nod. He was mildly surprised that he had not gone for the easy answer: the promise of a happy, healthy family. Shane was glad to have him as company.

Herbert kept the boy distracted as they continued walking. He told Jason stories about his days in the carnival and what he did in his act. He told him about other acts, and strange things he had seen, and at some point, he even got Jason to laugh.

The homes petered out three blocks down the road, and they came upon a vast, fenced-in lot that had been cut out of the surrounding forest. The property looked enormous, and more and more came into view as Shane approached, including a sign on a tower that read "Johnny's Scrapyard". A smell that he had only vaguely noticed before grew stronger the closer they got, like old eggs and dead things.

Massive stacks of scrap were piled three and four stories high and featured rusted bed frames, refrigerators, rebar, wires, ovens, water heaters, and a thousand other identifiable things.

More junk than the town of Burkitt could have produced in a century seemed to fill the corrugated aluminum walls of the scrapyard. The outside gate was bent outward as though something had escaped rather than broken in. The office building was located just to the left and featured broken windows and a collapsed roof. No one had been there in years.

The trio walked onto the property, and Shane looked at the ground. There was a path to the left around the office and then two roads into the scrap, one to the right and one right up the center. There were fresh tire marks in the dirt up the center path. Several of them. More than one vehicle had been that way since the last rainfall.

The towering scrap heaps made it impossible to tell what was waiting for them in any direction. The tire tracks seemed like the obvious lead, but now he was wondering if it was too obvious.

"What if we go up there?" Jason pointed at the giant scrapyard billboard and the rusty ladder that led up the side of the pole to the platform it was posted on.

"Not a bad idea," Shane said.

Herbert opted to stay on the ground rather than going ahead, to make sure nothing happened to Jason. Shane took the lead and climbed the rickety ladder, flakes of old paint and rust coming away in his grip. The task was more awkward than it should have been thanks to his broken finger, but he made it to the top and stood on the platform, looking out over the yard.

The piles of scrap were only at the front of the property. They stopped about forty yards in and were replaced by cars. They could have filled at least a few football fields. There were as many cars as Shane had ever seen. Fields and fields of automobiles haphazardly lined up and, in some cases, crashed together.

There were rusted heaps that looked like they were from the fifties and sixties, and newer vehicles as well, closer to the entrance. The majority looked like models from the seventies and eighties. Cars from when Burkitt was still a town with the living in it.

At the center of the lot lay another swamp, like the property had flooded and never dried out. Cars were half-sunk in mud and weeds alongside some serious heavy equipment like bulldozers and a few dump trucks.

For a moment, Shane thought he saw a torch or some kind of firelight, but it vanished.

A trick of the light, he thought. Or ghosts toying with them in the distance.

"That's our SUV." Jason pointed excitedly after joining Shane. It was down the center lane, as Shane had expected. It was also not the newest car in the lot.

Parked alongside the SUV were two state police cruisers that had to have been from the first response to the missing family. They were part of the reason the rest of the police were parked up the highway, fearful of entering the town.

"Let's go take a look," Shane said.

They began the climb back down.

CHAPTER 12

FAVORS

Metal groaned as they passed the towers of trash, and Shane suppressed the feeling he was walking into a trap. He had gotten a good look at what awaited them. Places to go in case they needed cover. Escape routes. There were options if things got ugly.

The trash piles had to be full of iron. It would be hard for spirits to try to get rid of them; at least that's what he told himself. It made him wonder how they got stacked so high in the first place, though. Maybe Johnny—whoever he was—had worked hard at it before Burkitt fell apart.

The creaks and whines of rusty steel could have been the product of the faint breeze, or even Shane and the boy walking past them. The ghosts of Burkitt had to be hiding somewhere, though.

They said little as they walked, Jason picking up on the tension from Shane as they made their way to where the cars had been dumped. Some, parked around the outskirts of the car graveyard, had visible remains inside. Skeletal bodies were slumped over steering wheels or hanging out of windows. The boy gave no sign if he saw them. He was focused on one thing.

Some of the cars were packed full of bags; old luggage, packages, and more, jammed in rear seats. These were people who were on road trips, Shane thought, or headed on vacation. The kinds of people who might take a wrong turn into Burkitt on their way to somewhere else and never found their way back.

The number of ghosts in town made more sense now. Not everyone from Burkitt had become spirits. The numbers had been supplemented, over the years, by as many travelers as the spirits could trap. There were hundreds of cars in the lot, maybe thousands.

If the spirits of Burkitt were skilled at creating illusions, if they could make the dead town seem alive, then it would be no trouble to make the dead town seem abandoned. To hide a lot full of cars and bodies if it came to that. No one investigating missing people would notice anything if the ghosts didn't want them to.

It made Shane wonder what they had walked into. Were the spirits building toward a simple cover-up again? The plan could have been to make Jason's family vanish, make some of the police vanish, and then wait for everyone to forget. Maybe the town would let the police come and search and turn up nothing. Maybe it would kill them all.

They kept walking, approaching the latest vehicles to join the scrap heap. As soon as they were in view, Jason bolted for his family car.

"Mom! Dad!" he yelled.

Shane gritted his teeth, biting back what he wanted to say. Jason was a child in a tough situation. He could remember that. For a while, anyway.

"Kid, keep it down," he urged. Jason was already in the vehicle. By the time Shane reached the SUV, he was sitting in the back seat with his head down. No one else was there.

"They're not there," Jason said. Shane nodded, looking over the inside of the vehicle. No sign of blood or a mess that might have indicated a fight. It was likely no one came back to the vehicle before it was moved.

"Shane," Herbert said loudly before he could respond to the boy.

The big ghost had stopped at one of the police cruisers. He stared over the roof of it at Shane, his expression grim.

"Wait here," Shane told Jason.

He didn't wait for the boy to answer before he walked away, joining Herbert at the state police cruiser. There was no need to ask the ghost what he wanted; it was clear as he approached what had caused him to call Shane over.

Two uniformed bodies were in the front seat of the car. The driver's throat and chest were gone, the flesh and much of the muscle tissue removed down to the ribs. The passenger had no head. There was no blood anywhere in the car. Not even a drop.

"How many cars are just like this one?" Herbert asked, looking across the lot. Somewhere in the distance came a sound, like a faint whistle, then a growling animal. It lasted only a few seconds and then stopped. Something was waiting.

"Most," Shane guessed.

"This place is Hell, Shane," Herbert whispered. "We need to get out of here."

"We will." Shane kept his voice low enough that Jason would not hear. "But we need to finish it."

"Even you can't stand up to this. Look at these men. Look at this lot!"

"It's like weeds in a garden, Herbert. They'll spread everywhere if you let them. You have to use weed killer."

Herbert stared at him in silence for a moment and then, despite the gravity of the moment, he let out a very quiet laugh.

"That was a good line. Did you just think of it?"

"Thought of it earlier," Shane admitted. "All the weeds around the houses when we got here."

Herbert sighed dramatically and nodded.

"We're weed killers, then. I'm just afraid it—"

"Don't be." Shane interrupted. "Fear won't get the job done. Plus—"

The sharp crackle of radio static stopped him from finishing the thought.

"Baker Two, this is dispatch. Come in, over."

The radio crackled with static again, and Shane bent down, looking inside the car.

"Baker Two, dispatch. Come back, over."

"Dispatch, Baker Two, was just grabbing coffee, over."

Shane looked up at Herbert, then reached into the car over the headless officer and took the receiver from the radio, pulling it out as far as the cord would allow.

"Be advised, Baker Two, additional units are ten minutes out, and you are on escort duty. Get your sugar and cream quick, Potter. Over"

"Dispatch, come on. Escort? For whom? Over."

"Federal agents, Potter. SWAT from Dover en route as well. Over."

Shane cursed and shook his head. He was afraid they were waiting for bigger guns. Federal agents and SWAT were definitely big. There was a chance Burkitt would let them pass unharmed and show them nothing. But there was as much chance everyone would die.

Shane dug in his pocket and pulled out his phone. Ventura had given Shane his number before they parted ways. He hadn't expected a need to call the man so soon—or ever, really—but if federal agents were already on the way, then he'd be their best chance to control things.

"Stay out of Burkitt or you're going to regret it," Shane said sharply into the mic for the radio before releasing the button with a burst of static. With his other hand, he dialed Ventura's number on his damp but still functional phone.

"What did you do that for?" Herbert asked.

"This is a restricted frequency. Please identify yourself," came the response over the radio.

"No. Stay out of Burkitt or you'll regret it," Shane said before dropping the mic.

"Might buy us a little more time if they think someone in town is up to no good," he told Herbert.

"They'll think it's a hostage situation," the ghost said in a way that suggested he didn't approve.

"Maybe," Shane agreed.

"Until they find their dead troopers and your fingerprints on the radio, then it'll be murder."

"No prints." Shane planned to wipe them clean.

The dispatcher kept talking over the radio as Shane walked away, phone to his ear.

"Agent Ventura," the man said through the phone.

"Ventura, it's Shane Ryan."

"Ryan. Didn't expect to hear from you so soon."

"Didn't expect I'd be stuck in a haunted town about to be raided by federal agents so soon," he explained.

"Jesus. Are you in Burkitt, Delaware?"

Shane chuckled.

"So, you're already on it?"

"Not on it, no. Not my case. But I caught wind about four hours ago. Family of four and six state troopers."

"This is where Lisette got her start," Shane said. "People here killed her son. This whole town is dead. I got two dead troopers in front of me, found one member of the family alive, and I'm guessing there are anywhere from a few hundred to a thousand angry spirits here."

Ventura didn't say anything for a long moment, but Shane could hear a keyboard clacking in the background.

"Thousand?" Ventura asked.

"Maybe. They've been growing them here like crops, probably for more than a century now."

"How is that possible?"

"We can hash it out over coffee later if I survive, but I need a hand making sure a SWAT team doesn't roll in here and level the town while I'm looking for that family."

"Already on it," Ventura said. "You said you found one of them?"

"Boy named Jason. He's twelve. Ghost was saving him for later. His mom and sister went off together when they thought the town was safe. Dad got taken by someone who calls himself the Magister."

"Means 'master' in Latin. Or 'teacher', I guess."

"Here, it means a ghost who likes killing," Shane said.

"It hasn't even been two days. How did you get yourself into another jam like this?"

"Same jam," Shane corrected. "Needed to tie up the loose ends, finish the ghost who started it. Turned out to be messier than I expected was all."

"I'm putting out a dispatch that I have an undercover agent on scene, and he has found one of the missing family members. That should give you some time to get out safely."

Shane grunted into the phone and looked back at the corpses in the car.

"Not looking to leave town yet," he explained.

"Ryan, come on."

"If they're here, I need to find them. And I need to get to the Magister or else another family rolls into town next week and this happens all over again. They'll cover it up. Your men will come in here, and everything will look fine. No bodies, no tracks, not a hair out of place. Or they all die. Either way, Burkitt wins. I have to make sure it loses."

"I don't have a lot of options, Ryan. I can't just tell people not to go into a town with 10 missing persons, six of whom are state police."

"You'll think of something. You're in the FBI; come up with something that'll terrify the locals and keep them in line."

"Terrorists? You want me to blame this on middle-of-the-woods Delaware terrorists?"

"I never said that. I said terrify," Shane clarified. "Just do it. The ghosts have changed things up since I got here. Something's brewing, and the less warm bodies in town, the better, until I figure out what's going on."

Ventura sighed over the phone, and more keys clicked.

"I'll try. I'm heading your way, though. Still haven't left New York after the hospital incident. I'll be there in a few hours."

"Don't come into town when you get here. Don't let anyone in."

"Got it. But I can't hold this for long without any evidence, especially with other agents on the scene. I doubt I can get you to sundown."

Shane looked at the sky and grunted again. He had a few hours at most.

After that, all hell was going to break loose.

CHAPTER 13

IN THE MURK

Shane hung up the phone and slipped it back in his pocket.

"Who was that?" Jason asked, sticking his head out of the SUV window. Herbert blocked the window to the police cruiser while Shane approached the boy.

"The FBI. We've got some backup on the way."

"Are they coming to find my mom and dad?"

"Not if we find them first," Shane said. "Remember, we don't want other people getting in the way or getting hurt."

He wished there was a way to get the boy to stay put, but that wouldn't work. He wouldn't listen to start; what twelve-year-old ever did? And the ghosts would certainly not leave him alone. They needed to get him out of town.

"Help!"

The cry came from somewhere in the distance and Shane whipped his head around, his eyes scanning the automobile graveyard. It was coming from the scrapyard.

"What was that?" Jason yelped.

Shane shushed him, holding a hand with a finger up but not looking down at the boy. He was not yet sure if it was a living person calling out.

"Help me!" the voice yelled again, muffled and distant.

"Hailey!" Jason shouted. He struggled to the far side of the SUV and opened the door, rushing out into the lot.

"Kid!" Shane shouted at him.

The boy stopped no more than ten paces away. His expression was one of doubt and fear. His desire to save his family was battling with his fear of what he had already seen and what might still be out there.

"We have to be smart here, right?" Shane said.

"Help!" the voice cried again.

The boy drew in a sharp breath and shook his head. Shane swore as he saw the resolve appear behind the anguish. He was twelve, but he was tougher than he looked. Maybe dumber than he looked, too. But he could hardly blame the kid.

Jason took off at a run and Shane growled. Herbert was already with him as they took off after the boy, running between and around cars, just trying to keep him in view.

A familiar laughter paced them, the same laugh they'd heard near the police station, and Shane swore again. Faces appeared in car windows, and hands crept over hoods and out from behind tires. The ghosts of Burkitt were creeping out of the dark places again, sensing a moment of discord.

"Kid!" Shane yelled.

The maze of cars was impossible to navigate without stopping and starting again and again. They were not parked in any logical order; some had simply been crashed together. What looked like a pathway would sometimes end with another car blocking the way, and the only choice was to backtrack or climb over the wreck. He lost sight of Jason after just a few moments.

"Help!" the voice called once more.

Jason had thought it was his sister, but Shane still couldn't tell if it was a trick. They might not know until they reached whoever or whatever was calling out. If there was even anything to reach.

A smell like sulfur and rotten vegetables grew thicker in the air as they drew closer to the swampy area in the center of the lot. The ground became muddy first and then standing water appeared.

Shane was forced to slow as the earth sucked at his boots, threatening to pull them off in the muck. Weeds and cattails grew around the edges of rusting cars, and bigger farm and construction machines replaced the smaller vehicles.

"Some of these are new," Herbert pointed out, passing a semi-truck missing its trailer. "Maybe within the past month."

"Yeah. Work never stops in Burkitt," Shane replied.

The voice had gone silent and there was no sign of Jason. Shane climbed onto the hood of a Toyota and stood, scanning the mire for any sign of movement.

"Jason," he yelled.

Dark water bubbled across the swamp. Shane watched as something stirred beneath the surface and grew more violent, the bubbles coming faster until a sound like a muffled whistle filled the air.

"What is that?" Herbert asked.

As if in answer, a sound like a deep, animal exhale preceded a burst of fire. Flames shot into the air as whatever gas beneath the surface vented, roaring like an enraged beast for perhaps thirty seconds before sputtering and going out. The water settled as though nothing had happened.

"That was unexpected," Herbert said.

The air reeked of methane and other chemicals.

"Remind me not to light a cigarette here," Shane said. Whatever gases were bubbling beneath the surface were volatile and probably deadly.

"Jason!" Herbert shouted. "It's not safe in here."

That was an understatement, and the dangers were increasing.

"Hello? We're here. We're in here!" came the reply, not from the boy but from the same voice that had drawn them in.

"Hailey!" Jason yelled, close but not in sight.

Shane watched shadows dart around sunken cars and under the surface of the swamp. Ghosts were swirling like piranhas.

"She's bait," Shane said, getting off the hood of the car.

He ran through the swamp, sinking into knee-deep muck as he headed toward the shouts.

"Keep talking so we can find you," Shane yelled.

"Here! Please help us," the girl yelled, still muffled but much closer now.

Another bubbling jet burst into flames on Shane's left. The light exposed the surrounding depths, as well as the bodies face-down in the water and mud. Some were whole, but many looked to be dismembered corpses tossed into the swamp.

"Shane, she's here!" Jason yelled.

Shane could not see the boy past the remains of a half-sunken garbage truck. He and Herbert made their way around it, wading into shallower water and more visible corpses. The smell of rot was stomach-turning now, and so thick he could feel it in the back of his throat. The only solace was that the dead had kept even insect life at bay and nothing had feasted or bred in the filth.

They rounded the truck and found Jason perched on the tailgate of a pickup, the front end lost in the mud. He was positioned over a car that Shane couldn't identify. Most of it was underwater and only the truck was above, itself nearly a third submerged.

Fire sputtered from a geyser on the boy's right, and he winced, ducking into the back of the truck with a scream. The whistling died out, and the flames went with it.

"Jason? Jason!" the voice yelled from the trunk.

"Wait," Shane shouted, pointing a finger at the boy as his head popped up from the flatbed. He waded deeper into the water, heading for the car until he reached the trunk, waist-deep in the swamp.

He could see spirits in the darkness, swimming near but not close enough to touch him. It reminded him of the dark ones in the cellar back home, darting about like rats. They were trying to sow fear more than anything else. If that was all they were up to, he'd let them have their fun.

Shane looked for a trunk latch but found nothing. His attempts to force it open proved useless.

"I need a pry bar or something," he said over his shoulder.

"Here!" Jason said, producing a tire iron from the back of the truck before Shane could even finish his request. The boy threw it, and Shane caught it with his good hand, giving the kid a nod of thanks.

"I'm going to pry it open. Hold on," Shane yelled at the trunk. He braced his feet in the muddy water and slammed the end of the bar against the seam of the trunk near the latch, putting his weight into it. He wished Herbert could put his weight on the iron to get the job done faster.

His broken finger sent shocks of pain up his arm as he wiggled and forced the bar under the trunk lid until he had it wedged. Shane pushed and lurched, gritting his teeth until metal snapped and the trunk lid popped open.

A girl of about sixteen stared up at him, her hair caked with mud and filth smeared across her face. Her eyes were wide and terrified. She held a woman in her arms, equally filth-covered in the partially submerged trunk and completely unconscious.

The girl was shaking, and she held fast to her mother as Shane stood over them with a tire iron in hand. She screamed and Shane tossed away the tool, holding up his hands.

"It's okay. You're okay," he told the girl.

"Hailey!" Jason yelled.

The boy leaped from the truck into the swamp and trudged over in nearly chest-deep water.

"Jason? Oh my god, Jason, what happened? What's happening?" his sister exclaimed.

The boy climbed into the trunk, and they embraced roughly.

"Mom?" Jason called out, trying to shake her awake.

"We need to get them out of here," Shane said, turning to Herbert. They'd waste hours trying to ask and answer questions; time which none of them had.

"Is the mother...?" Herbert began.

Shane leaned into the trunk, reaching for the woman's neck. Hailey screamed and pulled her mother and Jason back a few inches.

"It's okay! He's a friend. He saved me. He's going to save all of us," Jason told her.

"Shane Ryan," he said, nodding at the girl. "I just need to check your mom."

"She's alive," the girl said shakily. "She won't wake up, but she's breathing. I made sure she was breathing."

"That's good," Shane said. The woman's pulse was strong, but there was a bloody mass of hair and muck on the left side of her head. She had been hit with something hard.

"Please, you have to get us out of here. I don't know what happened. I don't know. I don't know what happened. I don't—"

"It's okay," Shane said, interrupting her. "Hailey, is it?"

"Hailey. Yes. Yes, sir," she said, her eyes still wide.

"Hailey, great. I'm getting you out of here. We need to be quick, though. I can answer questions later, but moving is the most important thing right now."

The water sputtered behind him, growing violent as the bubbling increased. Shane cursed and looked at Jason.

"It's gonna burn," the boy said. Shane nodded.

"Take your sister. I've got your mom," he said.

The boy climbed out into the water, dragging the girl with him. She protested at first, still terrified and in shock, until Shane pulled their mother from her arms, lifting her and turning away.

"Move," Shane instructed, stomping through the swamp. Jason pulled at his sister, and she eventually complied as the whistling rose in pitch and then belched a gout of fire into the air.

Hailey screamed and fell to her knees, but her brother kept pulling her. Cold air followed, and Shane looked over his shoulder at the fire. A figure stood in the blast of burning gas. When the flame died, the figure remained.

The ghost was that of a man. He wore overalls with no shirt, and there was severe bruising across his body. His wrists, elbows, shoulders, and neck were nearly black. His head hung slumped to the side.

As Shane reached dry ground, he set the children's mother on the hood of an old Ford. The overalls ghost followed them, his arms and legs bending the wrong way with each movement. All of his joints had been broken, Shane realized. Every single one of them.

"We don't like thieves," the ghost said, his head flopped back so that he was looking at the sky instead of Shane. His voice sounded like that of a chronic smoker holding back a cough with every syllable.

"Don't plan on stealing anything," Shane told him. "Just taking these people and leaving in peace."

Hailey was crying and her brother calmed her, telling her Shane was going to keep them safe, while Herbert stood between them and the encroaching spirit. Others circled in the junkyard, moving through the scrapped cars and swamp.

"No one steals from me. Or Magister. No one," the ghost said. It walked closer on wobbly legs, and Shane rolled his eyes.

"What are you going to do about it?"

CHAPTER 14
THE BROKEN MAN

The ghost jerked his body roughly and his head fell forward, lolling to one side. The man's face was a patchwork of scars and stubble. He looked at Shane and then Herbert.

"You're not from here," he said to the big ghost. "You don't know."

"Know what?" Herbert asked.

The broken ghost sucked air in through his teeth, a nervous habit from life, maybe.

"Magister will be angry. He runs Burkitt. Everything here is his. Everyone here is his. Even you, now."

"I'll be happy to correct his misunderstanding when I see him," Shane said.

The ghost exhaled a disappointed sound.

"I was cocky like you once," he said, his chuckle sounding more like a death rattle than genuine laughter. "Not so cocky now, am I?"

"You look like a man who knows how to lose a fight," Shane told him. That made the ghost laugh heartily. His entire body shook and swayed like he might fall apart, limb from limb, at any moment.

"Heh. As I was saying, he owns it all. He owns you. Accept your fate and maybe... maybe your death will be swift."

"You're not selling me on this Magister," Shane said. "Your sales pitch could use a lot of work."

The ghost hobbled forward another step as a new blast of flame rose behind him. His arms dangled like meat hanging in a butcher shop window, and his eyes were fixed on Shane's.

"You need to understand. He's stronger than ever, and now he's growing. It's time now. Time to expand. Time to make Burkitt spread."

"What does that mean?" Herbert asked. The broken man looked at him and smiled. The teeth in his mouth were as broken as his bones.

"We grow. We get bigger. Burkitt becomes… everything. Everywhere. Plant your flags out and out and out. Bigger and better."

The ghost chuckled, and Shane glanced at Herbert. There was a reason the map wasn't fitting what they were seeing the way it should have. The town had expanded. The swamp was larger, pushing deeper into the woods and beyond the established borders.

A ghost like the Magister, no matter how strong he was, could only influence the area around where he was rooted, the place where his haunted item held his spirit like a tether. But if he was killing more people, if he killed the entire town of Burkitt, and then travelers, and anyone who passed within the town limits, the haunting could expand.

The Magister was adding to his numbers to push the boundaries of the haunted town. Burkitt was getting larger while staying dead. He just needed to position other spirits farther and farther out. Getting enough of them branched out, like spokes around the central hub, would push the borders ever outward.

It was possible, given time, that Burkitt could reach Wallaceburg. The ghosts could kill that town just like they'd killed Burkitt, replace the living with the dead, and then do it again. But it was not something that happened quickly. It was glacial.

The Magister had worked on this for decades. And, Shane realized, it was probably all going according to plan. A ghost had the patience to wait generations, and this one had been doing just that. He could spread out bit by bit, kill more people, force more spirits under his thumb, and extend the range of his kingdom of the dead.

The Custodian suddenly made sense. Shane had not understood why the Magister was working with something so powerful and dark like they were teammates. It was because they were. He allowed the Custodian to have the children and rule in the school because he was a lieutenant in his army.

The Custodian could push outward, could rule farther afield, and spread Burkitt's dark influence. There were likely other spirits who would do the same, their haunted items positioned around town to push the borders farther out.

"Are you one of his soldiers? In making Burkitt bigger? Is this your base?" Shane asked.

The ghost wheezed and laughed.

"We have to go, Jason!" Hailey said suddenly.

She was trying to pull her brother away, to sneak off while everyone was distracted, but the boy was not willing to go with her. The broken ghost saw them past Herbert and lifted a shaky arm, bent and busted in numerous places. He pointed a crooked finger at Jason.

"You. You are the Custodian's," he said. The boy froze and his sister did as well.

"No one's going to need to worry about the Custodian again," Shane said.

The broken ghost gazed at him and then laughed louder than ever, a deep belly laugh that forced him to close his eyes and nearly collapse.

"You saying you destroyed him?" the ghost asked between laughs. "Yeaaah, nah."

"We did," Herbert answered.

"Oh, Magister'll hate that so much. He'll be enraged," the ghost said, laughing even more. "He never shows it, you know? Never raised his voice, but I know he hates it when someone leaves. No one leaves unless he says so. And the Custodian was his favorite."

He stumbled forward, still chuckling to himself, and walked right past Shane and the unconscious woman.

"Come. Out of the swamp. This way," the ghost encouraged. His legs buckled and bowed, but he stayed upright as he led them away from the mud. Shane and the others stayed behind until the ghost stopped to look back.

"Please, come. Come! I'll tell you what I can. Bring the woman, get away from these spies and monsters."

Shane looked at Herbert, and the ghost shrugged.

"Jason. Hailey. Stay close," Shane said. He plucked their mother from where he had rested her and followed the ghost. Herbert followed the children, and they left the graveyard of cars, along with the many watching eyes.

"My name is Johnny, but most people called me Lucky when I was alive," the ghost said, taking them back to dry earth and down a new, untrodden path through the scrap. "It was kind of a joke."

"I bet," Shane said. "Where are we going, Lucky?"

"Just here," the ghost answered, leading them to a camper. The rear was open and there was a bed inside, relatively clean and empty, all things considered. The gear from whoever once owned it was still inside. Shane didn't bother to look in the front to see if any bodies were there. He placed the children's mother on the bed.

"There's food." Lucky pointed to the bags. "Cans and boxes and things... do you remember steak?"

He looked at Herbert when he asked, but Herbert did not reply.

"I used to love steak," the broken ghost continued.

Shane pulled open the bags and looked through. There were canned goods, juice boxes, and other snacks. He tossed some juice to Jason and a box of cereal bars to his sister.

"Eat something."

"What about my mom? She needs a hospital!" Hailey said. Her fear had dissipated somewhat, or her shock had let her push it aside. Either way, she was more focused now.

"We'll get her help soon," Shane said.

"You gotta trust him, Hale. He saved me from a monster." Jason gave her sister a bottle.

"That's a monster," his sister shouted, pointing at Lucky.

"Magister," Lucky corrected, looking at the children. "That's your monster."

"Where did he come from?" Herbert asked.

Lucky swayed like a breeze was working against him, and he watched the children open their cereal bars and eat.

"He didn't come from anywhere. That house was here before anyone else. Burkitt was built around it. He's always been here."

"Like a founding father or something?" Shane asked. Lucky shrugged.

"Something like that. You don't ask him questions. You don't protest, and you don't resist. You do what you're supposed to do. Or else."

"He destroys spirits?" Herbert asked. The concept of destroying the dead was still relatively new to him, but he was getting the hang of it.

Lucky's eyes were still fixed on the children, watching them with an uncomfortable intensity as they ate.

"Magister doesn't destroy anything. Just changes it. Living changes to dead. Dead changes to power."

His words were soft now like he was lost in a daydream. Herbert stepped in front of the children, blocking the ghost's view.

"What does that mean?"

"He consumes them," Lucky said, undeterred. He stared at Herbert's bulk as though seeing through him. "He eats them and makes them part of himself."

It was not a surprise to learn that the Magister consumed other spirits. Not to Shane, at least. Strong ones could feed on the weak. It wasn't literal eating, but "consuming" was a reasonable description. Absorbing. Taking their power to grow stronger and deadlier.

"Sounds like he's the sort of guy who bit off more than he can chew," Shane said. Lucky blinked and finally turned to look at him, chuckling once more.

"He's going to hate you so much," the ghost said.

"The feeling is mutual."

"Many of the spirits here willingly do what he says. The Custodian did. The Custodian loved Magister. Like an obedient hound waiting to be thrown a bone all the time, he was. There are others. But most? No, not most."

"Trouble in paradise then, huh?" Shane asked.

"Not trouble. Just... dissatisfaction. There is no civil war brewing, but most do not agree with him. Do not support him. They just do what they have to do to appease him."

"Which is what? Kill travelers?" Shane gestured to the abandoned vehicles in the lot.

"Yes," Lucky answered. "Kill or be killed. It is not a hard choice for most."

"There's always a choice," Herbert argued.

"Is there? Go to the house and you'll see. We're all there. Our bones. Our coins. Our wedding rings. The things that hold us all. He keeps them there, close to him. Under his watch. No one dared argue with him. We have no way to escape," Lucky explained.

"Your haunted items are all there? All in the same house?" Shane asked.

"Except for his favorites. The Custodian's. Hunter's. Biter's. Runner's. Theirs get moved. Like I told you. Pushing out. Making Burkitt bigger."

"And you? You're not a lieutenant out here?"

"No," Lucky said, shaking his head. "I used to own this scrapyard. Long ago. Was not nearly as big as it is now. Not nearly so crowded. They came for me in the night. I was listening to my radio about the Soviets. Just launched their space thing then, their Sputnik, you know? And then the radio went dead, and the lights, too. They came, and they broke me, piece by piece. Little bit by little bit, right in my home."

"Who did?" Herbert asked.

"Magister. His helpers. Shadows was all I saw at first. Broke my fingers. Broke my toes. Broke my ankles. Broke my wrists. Crack and snap and crunch. And I hoped it would hurt less the next time, but it never did. Never went numb or faded away. Not even once."

"I think he makes it hurt to make a ghost more likely to happen," Shane said, as much to Herbert as Lucky. "Suffering helps make the dead return. It's no guarantee, but it ups the chance."

"He's right," Lucky said, chuckling again. "Know why he did it? Why me, specifically? Know what he said to me after?"

The ghost's voice was very quiet now, and the sense that he might laugh again was long gone. Shane only shook his head.

"Nothin'. He never said anything to me again, never in all these years. Never gave me a job. Never said my name. It was for nothin'."

"Does he have a plan? An endgame for all this death?" Shane asked.

"Burkitt." Lucky grinned his broken grin. "He wants to inch the borders of Burkitt out and out and out. He wants everything to become Burkitt one day, and he can be in charge."

"Everything?" Herbert asked incredulously. "How could that ever happen?"

"He's been dead a very long time, friend. Time doesn't mean anything to him. If it takes a thousand years, ten thousand years, do you think he cares? He wants to cover everything, everywhere, and take every life he can until all that remains are the spirits he controls."

"It's impossible. Absurd," Herbert protested. Lucky chuckled again.

"Is it?" he said. "Makes you wonder."

"How long has he been here?" Shane asked. "How old is that house?"

"This is Delaware. His people settled here before America was even a country."

"He's been doing this for nearly two hundred and fifty years?"

Herbert looked at Shane as if hoping for clarification or refutation. Shane had none to give.

Shane had encountered spirits that were that old and older, but none that had such an ambitious plan. Few seemed to have the patience of the Magister, if that was truly his intent. He was moving very slowly. But Lucky was right.

Even if it took a thousand years, what difference did it make to someone who was already dead? If anything, it played into his hand. The slow creeping of Burkitt would be much harder to notice if it forever looked like an empty, dead town, even as it consumed other towns. In the sleepy backwoods of Delaware, few people would notice.

"He won't let anything in the world stop him," Lucky added.

He did not laugh after he said it.

CHAPTER 15
RUN FOR YOUR LIFE

Jason and his sister continued to eat and rest by their mother's side while Herbert kept watch. None of the swamp ghosts had approached, and Lucky said they would not. He said they stayed in the swamp exclusively unless the Magister told them to do something else. And if the Magister showed up, they'd all be dead, by now. He was very confident in the Magister's abilities.

"Why were they kept alive?" Shane asked, nodding to the children.

"You already know," Lucky replied. "He takes his time."

"So, he never kills just for pleasure."

"No. Why waste the potential?" the ghost replied. "He takes his time all the time. He likes them... seasoned."

It made a perverse sense. The children and their mother were saved because killing them too quickly would waste the kill. Waste their suffering. The Magister wanted ghosts. Prolonging the fear and pain for as long as possible increased his odds of a good final product. He was making artisanal ghosts.

Shane stepped away from the camper, gesturing for Lucky to come with him. He walked several steps, slowly and casually, until he was confident there was enough distance between them and the kids.

"Their father was taken into the house. So was the boy, but the Custodian got him. Is the man still alive?" Shane whispered.

Lucky swayed and hummed. He might have been trying to shake his head, but it was hard to tell.

"No way to know. Like I said, he likes to take his time. He's kept people alive for weeks. They were mad by the end, sick with infection, and too weak to move. But he made sure they were alive. Though sometimes, he works on them faster."

"Is there a way into the house?" Shane asked.

"Lots of ways in. None out," Lucky told him.

"I'll worry about that later. I just need to know how to find the Magister and get this finished."

"You can't surprise him. He already knows you're here. Will probably know every word of this conversation in a matter of minutes. There are too many ghosts working for him. You'll never catch him off-guard."

"He doesn't need to be off-guard. He just needs to be close."

"Then he won't be," Lucky explained. "If you need to lay hands on him, he'll watch you from afar as the others peel the flesh from your bones. He doesn't lose because he can't. He's dead and you're not. He always has the upper hand."

"A lot of others have thought the same way. I'm still here, though."

"I wish you luck, then. But I won't be surprised when I see your ghost back here when he's done with you."

Shane smirked turned to head back to the camper.

If the Magister knew he was coming, then coming up with a strategy was useless. Shane needed a plan, but there were only so many ways to prepare to fight a powerful spirit who already knew he was coming. It didn't sound like he would have much luck trying to scout the town or the house. Not with a hundred ghost spies between him and the Magister.

The children were another problem. He couldn't take them deeper into the town. It would be too hard to keep them safe, and they had their unconscious mother to deal with. They needed to get out of Burkitt, but Shane wasn't willing to leave yet.

"What do you guys say we get your mom to some help?" Shane asked, joining the others.

"We're leaving?" Hailey asked hopefully, dropping a half-eaten cereal bar.

"Yeah. Quick, though. I don't think everyone's going to be happy to see us go."

Shane lifted their mother's unconscious body, holding her awkwardly until he found a position that didn't hurt his finger.

"I thought we couldn't leave?" Herbert asked in a low voice.

"Can't think of another option. And it's just them. I'm coming back. With you, if you're still in."

"Of course," Herbert said. "But the FBI—"

"—was told there's a man undercover in town. So, when I rescue these three people, I'll tell them I'm going back for their dad."

"You know where our dad is?" Hailey grabbed Shane's arm. Jason stood at her side, looking hopeful yet terrified.

"Your brother told me where to look. So, you guys are going to take care of your mom while I go back for him."

"I want to come with you," Jason said. "I know the way."

Shane almost laughed. The kid was brave, he had to give him that. Maybe not the brightest idea, but adrenaline and fear made you do weird things.

"I know the way too, kid. And I don't know how to keep an eye on your mom and your sister, so that's your job. Plus, let's be honest, you don't really want to come."

"I do," the boy protested.

"No, you don't. I don't want to go, either. This place is a nightmare."

"You stay with me, Jason. Mom would kill me if I lost you again," Hailey said to her brother.

"Good. Settled. Let's go."

Shane gave Lucky a nod and started walking, Herbert and the children following closely behind. The broken ghost watched them with a frown.

"He won't let you leave. He never does," Lucky said.

"About time he got used to disappointment," Shane said over his shoulder. The Magister had spent too much time in the backwoods by himself. He had grown too smug.

They left the scrapyard, heading back toward the main street. Shane carried the unconscious woman while the children and Herbert joined him at his side. His plan was a simple path, up the street and out of town to the police blockade. They'd stick to the open road, away from the buildings. Even if the ghosts were watching, they'd have to make a move and expose themselves first.

"Shane," Herbert said, his tone anxious.

They had barely passed the boundaries of the scrapyard. A ghost in the window of the nearest house stared out at them, pale white face pressed to the glass and eyeless sockets watching.

"Oh, my God," Hailey whimpered, catching sight of the spirit.

"Just look forward," Herbert suggested. "Ignore them."

"I don't understand what's happening here," the girl said.

"It's ghosts," her brother said, taking her hand. "It's a bunch of ghosts, but Shane fights them, and so does Herbert, even though he is one."

"Oh, my God!" the girl said again. Her brother squeezed her hand.

"They're good guys. You'll see. Just keep going."

"Yeah. Keep going," she agreed, keeping her eyes on the road.

Spirits crept from the houses nearby, some slithering like shadowy snakes across porches, others pushing through the overgrown weeds and shrubs.

Shane ignored them all, though he took stock of every movement in his peripheral vision. There had been none on their way in, and he wasn't sure if they had all been in hiding or if the Magister had moved them in from elsewhere.

The woman he carried was not heavy, but the distance was considerable, and her weight seemed to grow with every step. His broken finger throbbed, and he found himself clenching his teeth and breathing heavily well before they reached the main street.

"Are you okay?" Herbert asked him.

Sweat ran down Shane's head, and he nodded. There was no way the children could carry her, nor could Herbert. And if he left her behind, Shane knew he'd never find her again. He had to press on.

Whispers came from the houses and shapes came closer, advancing across the lawns, and hiding behind trees. There was still so much ground to cover.

Shane picked up the pace, forcing his muscles to work. His legs felt like fire, but he pushed onward. He adjusted the unconscious woman's position, tossing her over his shoulder in a fireman's carry position, hoping he wasn't causing extra damage to the wound on her head by doing so.

The adjustment provided some relief, but it was short-lived. Within a block, he was feeling the fatigue as strongly as ever. He had not given himself a chance to rest since pursuing and fighting Lisette.

He should have been smarter and taken more time, but he wanted it over with. After the time and distance he and Herbert had covered, after being pursued by the law and the dead, he was just too eager to put the final nail in the coffin. Then he walked into something bigger than he'd expected.

"Hold on," Shane said, coming to a stop. Ahead of them on the road, a single dark figure waited. It was not a living man.

"Who is that?" Jason asked.

"Doesn't matter," Shane replied. The ghosts of Burkitt had put them in a standoff.

"Let me take her," Herbert suggested, looking at the woman over Shane's shoulder.

"You can't," Shane told him.

"I can. I saw Linskey do it back at Bartolomy's a few times. It was a trick he did for fun."

Possession, Shane thought. She was unconscious, so it would not be hard for the ghost to take control.

A second spirit appeared on the road, joining the first. Shane cursed. There was no time to think of something better. They needed to be quick.

"Do it," he said, crouching to lay the woman on the road.

"Do what?" Hailey asked. "What's happening?"

"We need to get you kids and your mom out of here, so Herbert's going to help her out. Just until you're safe," he explained.

"What does that mean?" the teenager asked, panic seeping into her voice again. Herbert stood over the woman and fell back as though flopping into a pool. Hailey screamed and covered her mouth and then he was gone.

Their mother sat up and drew a deep breath.

"Mom?" Hailey said, stunned.

"Herbert?" Jason asked.

The woman turned her head and looked at them.

"It's Herbert," he confirmed in a woman's voice. She was much shorter than the real Herbert, and thinner. She looked like the sort of mom who liked to take her kids to soccer practice and have snacks ready when they got home from school.

"Take them," Shane said, helping Herbert to his feet. The woman nodded and looked at the kids.

"Okay, guys, I think we're going to need to be fast here."

"As fast as you can," Shane added.

They were just one block from the main street now. The run would be tiring, but they could make it. Shane could fight any ghosts that pursued. He had to.

"Follow me as closely as you can," Herbert told the children. He nodded at Shane, who broke into a run first.

The two ghosts on the street had not anticipated being attacked at a full run. They likely had not anticipated an attack at all, and that was Shane's hope. He slipped his hand into his pocket, finding the iron rings within, and forced them over a finger on each hand.

The first spirit, cloaked in shadow, hesitated as Shane backhanded it across the face. The iron hit ghostly flesh, and the spirit was forced from the road, back to the object that bound it. Lucky had said they were all in the Magister's house. By keeping them close, he had made it harder for them to pursue Shane and the others.

Shane's fist hit the other ghost in the gut, producing the same reaction.

"Long way to go," he shouted at Herbert and the others.

There were no more ghosts in the way, but there were more coming from the homes they passed.

CHAPTER 16
OUT

The road out of Burkitt led up a hill through the trees and then beyond what could be seen from the town. From the edge of the main strip, it looked like the road slowly rose into the sky and then stopped, like nothing existed beyond Burkitt.

The path was clear, and Shane knew that the police blockade waited not far beyond the rise. They had cut into the woods and circled to the swamp only a short distance beyond that. Now all they had to do was get back.

The children were compliant, their legs moving even if neither was ready to accept that their mother was now possessed by the ghost of a giant, carnival sideshow act of a man.

"Run and don't look back," Herbert ordered in the woman's voice. They did as they were told.

Shane was paces behind them, running only as fast as the others could to make sure he stayed between them and the town. For a long moment, the sound of shoes hitting pavement was the only sound in Burkitt.

But only for a moment.

There was no wind to feel, but the howl that rose from the town sounded like it was coming from the ruins of an old building, cutting through cracks and holes and resonating louder and louder.

Jason turned his head to look back but Herbert caught his face, the mother's hand touching his cheek as they ran.

"Don't," he said, firmly but not angrily. Jason looked at his mother, knowing it wasn't her, and nodded. He ran as fast as he could.

The windless howl became a roar. Shane felt cold air licking at his heels.

"Noooooooooooooo!"

The roar formed the word slowly and awkwardly, like a beast unused to human speech. The cold stung Shane's back, creeping across his neck and shoulders. He clenched his fists, letting the pain in his broken finger sear up his arm to feed his focus and rising anger.

"Keep going, Herbert," Shane ordered.

The children's mother looked over her shoulder as she ran. Her eyes widened, but she did not slow. Instead, she put a hand on the children's backs and pushed them harder. Then Shane looked back.

The road behind them was being swallowed by darkness as though someone was erasing it from existence, fragment by fragment. The pavement beneath their feet, the trees that walled them in, and even the sky above; darkness was consuming it all. It was like a great snake made of shadow had unhinged its jaws and was swallowing the road out of town.

At the forefront of the rush, a handful of spirits raced ahead of the surging darkness. Shane could make out arms and faces and whispered threats from a dozen enraged voices.

He reached into his pocket while he ran. He had slowed his pace just slightly, enough to let Herbert and the children widen the gap. He wanted the ghosts focused on him more than them. He just needed to buy a few minutes.

"I hear no one ever leaves this town," Shane shouted, pulling a small parcel from his pocket, the same bag he had retrieved from his trunk just before entering the woods outside of Burkitt.

The ghosts howled and hissed and cursed. He nodded, opening the bag and then slowing to a dead stop. The darkness swarmed over him, swallowing him in bitter cold. He could see nothing. All he could hear was the thundering roar like a freight train.

"Say hi to the Magister," Shane shouted over the roar.

He dumped the bag into his hand and then swung his fist in an arc, opening his hand with his palm out.

Iron shavings flew from one side of the road to the other, scattered like rice at a wedding. The darkness broke apart instantly, the roaring snapped to silence, and the cold was sucked into nothing.

Every spirit hit by the tiny metal flakes was forced back to the center of town, back to the Magister's house where he kept his slaves under his watchful eye. Only a trio of ghosts remained on the road, those fortunate enough to have been missed by the iron spray.

Shane approached the nearest of them, a hobbling spirit with one arm and a broken face, and punched it flat in the nose. He spun to make his way to the second ghost.

"Wait!" the spirit cried out, a tall, stocky man with bloody knuckles and no lips on his face. Shane's ring clipped him on the chin, the result of a swift uppercut, and the ghost disappeared like the others. Only one remained.

The ghost was on the side of the road near the edge of the trees. It was slinking away as if trying to remain unseen though it had no cover. It was thin and lithe and looked like it had once been an elderly woman.

"He made us come. He made us!" she protested. Shane lashed out, a backhand to the shoulder that she tried to deflect, and she was gone as well.

He knew the reprieve would be short. He could already see more spirits stirring back at the edge of town, but it was not clear if they were mounting another pursuit. He didn't wait around to see.

Herbert and the children had crested the hill. The children vanished and their mother paused for only a moment. Shane waved and started running. The woman turned and ran as well.

Running had never been Shane's favorite activity, but he had run far and drilled hard during his time in the Marines and could probably sleep with his legs moving if he had to. He ran up the hill after the others. His lungs stung, and he could feel sweat beading, but he pushed harder to catch up.

He was nearing the top of the rise where the blockade would come into view when something snagged his ankle, pulling Shane's leg out from under him.

He barely had time to shield his face from slamming against the pavement before he hit it with a grunt. Something scrambled onto his back, pinning him face-down on the road. He struggled to break free, but the ghost held him firmly. Ice-like claws gripped his wrists and kept his hands in place.

"You are a problem," a voice hissed in his ear, so close that he could nearly feel the spirit's lips.

"Been called worse," he replied.

"Who are you? Who thinks he can come and take what Magister owns?"

"Name's Shane. Really nice to meet you," he said, his face pressed to the gritty road. He could only see the trees to his left and sky in his peripheral vision. The ghost on his back kept itself out of sight.

"They say you killed the Custodian and freed all his little toys. I don't believe it. You are just a man… just a corpse waiting to happen."

"Yeah, you're probably right," Shane said between gritted teeth. "Hardly worth your time when you think about it."

The claws clamped down harder on his wrists. Shane could see bloody flesh on the ghost's arms but little else.

"What if I grated your face off on the road right here? What if I scoured you down to the bone, down to your brains?"

"I think the Magister would disapprove," Shane replied. If he was as the others had said, he wasn't keen on wasting bodies that he could warp into ghosts.

The spirit hissed into Shane's ear.

"Maybe Magister won't know," it whispered. Shane grinned.

"I don't think you believe that," he said. "I think you're a good little dog who serves his master."

The ghost growled and shifted its weight. Shane could feel it weighing down his back, looming over his head. He moved with it, turning his head, and slamming it against his attacker. He felt something crunch against his skull and the weight lifted off him as the ghost fell to one side.

Shane got to his knees and then back on his haunches as he pivoted, getting a look at the ghost. He was small and gangly, covered in patches of torn flesh and burns. The hair on his head had been burned and only a cap of melted hair remained, fused to the left side of his head.

The ghost held his mouth and then pulled away, revealing missing teeth that Shane had knocked loose.

"It's a good look," Shane said as he adjusted his ring.

The ghost hissed and ran at him. Two more spirits came from the trees, running to join the fight.

"You're like roaches," Shane said.

The ghost kicked out but Shane was ready and avoided the attack. One punch to the back of the head and the iron ring did its job, banishing the spirit to where it came from.

"You guys aren't tired of losing yet?" Shane asked the two others.

The spirit on the left was about his size but had a caved-in face. Eyes, nose, and mouth were replaced by the crushed mass of flesh and bone. The other was stockier and older. He looked like the sort of guy who retired to play golf on weekends.

"No one leaves Burkitt," the faceless ghost said. Shane could only shrug.

"Things change."

The ghosts separated, flanking Shane as they approached. He backed away slowly toward the trees, his fists ready, and kept both in view as he did so.

The faceless ghost moved an arm, and wind whipped through the trees. A branch broke and fell across Shane's hand, hitting his broken finger. He growled as pain ran up his arm like an electric shock. The ghosts were on him in an instant, each taking an arm.

Faceless had pinned Shane against a tree. The other ghost pressed Shane back, allowing Faceless to hold Shane with the tree between them, arms outstretched and pulled back in the spirit's grip.

"Things don't change," the older ghost said. "Not here."

CHAPTER 17
UNTO THE BREACH

The ghost leaned close to Shane's face and smiled.

"Magister is going to break you for what you've done," he said. "For what you did to the Custodian."

"I gather they were close," Shane said. The faceless ghost pulled harder on his arms, stretching them against the tree, and he winced.

"And even though he needs you alive, it doesn't mean he needs you whole."

"No?" Shane said. "I'm probably more impressive whole."

"Your tongue, for instance. I don't think it's needed. You're better off without it."

He took Shane's face in his hand and held it steady, scowling as he lifted his other hand. Shane resisted, for the sake of appearance, by trying to shake his head left and right. The ghost squeezed his face tighter.

"Nothing's saving you this time," the ghost warned. He clamped hard on the sides of Shane's jaw. His fingers were like ice, and they forced Shane's mouth open. The scowl became a grin as he lifted his free hand and pushed two fingers into Shane's mouth.

The ghostly digits felt like old, dead meat, cold and firm to the touch as they wriggled past Shane's teeth looking for his tongue. He bit down as hard as he could, and the ghost bellowed in surprise. He jerked his head left and right like a dog and shook the ghost's hand.

Instinctively, the ghost yanked his hand away just as Shane pulled hard to the left. The fingers came off in his mouth. The ghost shrieked, holding up his maimed hand as Shane spit the fingers back at him. They sailed through the air, end over end. No longer a part of the whole, there was nothing to keep them together and make them real. The fingers dissipated like morning fog under the rays of the sun and vanished before they hit their target.

"I'll gut you," the ghost growled.

"Good luck trying," Shane said, nodding to the spirit's right.

The ghost turned to face the road just in time to see the massive shape of Herbert crashing into it.

Herbert slammed the ghost to the ground under his bulk and then rose, lifting the spirit with him. Herbert then raised the ghost over his head and hurled him back the way he'd come, just as Faceless released Shane and came around the tree.

"Hey, you don't have a face."

The ghost turned toward Agent Ventura, who brought a length of iron bar down on the faceless head like he was hammering in a nail. The ghost vanished without a sound.

"You made it," Shane said, rubbing his wrists. Ventura nodded.

"Just, actually."

"This one's not done," Herbert pointed out. The ghost he had thrown had recovered and was coming back at them.

"I got him." Shane spit. Even though there was no real taste in his mouth, the feeling was objectionable, and he had the memory of something rancid.

"Need this?" Ventura offered the bar.

"No iron for this guy," Shane said with a shake of his head.

"It doesn't matter how many of you come; you will all—"

Shane removed his ring before punching the ghost in the mouth. He stumbled back on the road and Shane hit him again on the side of the head, then in the ear. A kick to the knee caused him to collapse.

Without another word, Shane dropped his knees onto the ghost's back and grasped his head in both hands. The ghost braced himself to push off the ground, a wasted effort. Shane twisted and then crushed in one fluid motion, breaking the ghost's neck and forcing his weight down on the skull.

The burst of power knocked Shane back toward Ventura and Herbert, and he landed on his back with a grunt.

"Jesus," Ventura said, giving him a hand. "Are you okay?"

"Is that all of them?" Shane asked, lifting his head to look around. Herbert scanned the forest and the road.

"I think so," he said.

"Then I'm fine," Shane replied, taking the agents hand to sit up. "How are the kids?"

"With EMTs," Ventura said. "Their mother suddenly fell unconscious after bringing them in. That was a hell of a show."

"It was my first time," Herbert said. Watching him climb out of the woman's body was probably not something Ventura had expected to see.

"Same," Ventura told him.

"Like a budding romance," Shane said. "Is she okay, though?"

"In and out," Ventura replied. "Head trauma and some blood loss, but they think she's going to be okay. I didn't stick around to hear a lot of details. You've got me working on a tight timeline here."

"How'd you explain running down the road with an iron bar in your hand?" Shane asked.

"I'm a federal agent; I don't explain myself to state troopers."

Shane grunted. It was as good an explanation as any.

"Got more gear, too," Ventura added, a little too excitedly. He unbuttoned his suit jacket and opened it up, revealing a vest inside covered in small metal studs.

"Iron?" Shane asked.

"Of course," he said. "Just like these."

Ventura reached into his pockets and pulled out a pair of leather gloves. They were studded with iron rivets just like the vest, across the back of the hand, the knuckles, and even the palms.

"Someone's been busy," Shane said.

"Had them in my trunk at the hospital. Just an idea I was toying with. I might not be able to pop off a ghost's head like a dandelion, but I can make them think twice about trying to take me on."

Shane was impressed with the hard work if nothing else. Ventura couldn't fight ghosts; he could only see them. But he was geared up enough to be helpful in a fight if it came to that.

"So, I'm here. I've got the locals holding off on an attack, and I need to know what's happening in there," the agent said, nodding toward the middle of town.

"Yeah," Shane said, flexing his hand. "It's haunted."

"Brilliant," Ventura replied. "Case closed, then."

"It's *really* haunted, Ventura. Sounds like this Magister has been running things in here since frontier times. He's got a custom ghost operation going on. It was the townspeople first, and when he ran out of them, he moved on to travelers and strays, whoever they could catch off the highway. He captures them, tortures them for as long as it takes, kills them, and then controls them when they come back as ghosts."

"Ghosts can do that?" Ventura said, staring toward the edge of town. The shadows were still there, a few random spirits, but none approached. The Magister had to be plotting a new attack. Or maybe he was just waiting for Shane to leave and cutting his losses.

"This one can. I heard he's trying to expand. The borders of Burkitt have been slowly moving outward as more ghosts fill the town. He wants to spread. Kill more. Make more residents."

"Slowly?" Ventura said.

"Already been at it for more than two hundred years. Seems keen to take a few hundred more if he needs to."

Ventura ran a hand through his hair and paced the road.

"I... how do I report this? What am I supposed to say?"

"Nothing yet. If the Magister gets destroyed, none of that matters anymore."

"*If.* And what about the father? Mitch Ansel?"

"He's with the Magister, as far as the kid knows," Shane answered.

"Okay, but is he alive? Dead? Ghost? What's happening?"

Shane sighed and watched Ventura pace until the man finally stopped, conscious that Shane was watching him.

"I don't know," Shane said. "There's no intel gathering in there. We got a quick rest in a junkyard with a ghost who was fed up with the Magister; that was it. Nothing is safe in Burkitt. There's no way to approach the Magister's house without him knowing, so when I go in, it's going to be blind."

"Then don't go in. I can lead a team—"

"Ventura, come on," Shane interrupted. "What team will be safe in there?"

"What's he going to do, attack an entire SWAT team? He'd be crazy."

"He's dead," Herbert pointed out. "He doesn't care."

"You can't think about this like he's got something to lose. If he killed every cop here, what would that mean to him? Do you actually think he'd be worried about getting exposed? Are you going to be the agent who goes on TV and blames the deaths of two dozen cops on ghosts?" Shane went on.

Ventura started pacing again, squeezing his gloves tightly, and staring out in the distance as though that might help him come up with an angle.

"The fewer people dealing with this, the better. You're still new to this; you need to trust me," Shane said.

"Yeah, but I still have six officers and one civilian missing. As far as anyone knows, this is a hostage situation. Hostages get taken by people. Criminals. Living criminals."

"Two of those cops are already dead. I don't know about the rest. I hear he likes to keep them alive, like that family. They might still be in there, and maybe I'm your hostage negotiator. Can you sell that?"

"No," Ventura said. "A hostage negotiator no one's heard of who sneaked into town and isn't on the books?"

"Then think of something to keep those cops out. Please," Shane said.

Ventura shook his head and swore, pacing even faster. He held a hand to his face, covering his mouth as he lost himself in thought, and then he finally stopped, looking at Shane's legs.

"What is this muck? The kids were covered in it too."

"Swamp in the center of the junkyard," Shane answered.

"It stinks like chemicals."

"Yeah, weird gas pockets or something. They light on fire at random. Is that helpful?"

"It is. I mean, it's stupid, but I can use it," Ventura told him. He pulled a radio from his belt and lifted it, looking at Shane as he held it to his mouth.

"Foster, this is Ventura. You there?"

"Go for Foster," a voice replied with a quick, static crackle.

"Foster, I need you to get the locals to lock down this perimeter and follow quarantine procedures. We have a chemical and maybe a biohazard in Burkitt."

The radio was silent for a beat and then crackled again.

"You wanna say that again?" Foster said.

"Chemical spill and possible biohazard in the town of Burkitt. We need immediate quarantine. No one in or out until I have word from Quantico and experts on scene. Copy?"

The silence was longer, and when the radio crackled again, it was a new voice.

"Agent Ventura, this is Chief Pike. What in the hell are you talking about? Quarantine? For what goddamn reason? My men are in that town!"

"Chief Pike, there is a possible chemical or biohazard on scene. If you want to go smell those kids' clothes, be my guest, but I suggest you wear a mask and gloves. I need you to alert the hospital. Keep them under observation, and I will call in a team to investigate. Your men are in town, and they will be found as soon as I can ensure that no one looking for them will have their skin melt off as they die screaming. Understood? Give the radio back to Foster."

He lowered the radio and grinned at Shane.

"Good?" he asked.

"Biohazard? Huh." Shane shrugged. "Works for me."

"Go for Foster," the voice on the radio interrupted.

"You get all that?" Ventura asked.

"Sure did. You coming back this way or—"

"Not yet. Gotta check a few things first," he replied.

Ventura replaced the radio on his belt.

"That'll buy you the better part of a day. A team has to be sent from the CDC to investigate. It's going to mean a lot more people, though, so when they do get here, if you're not done, then this thing will blow up," he said.

"So, I've got another twenty-four hours?"

"At best. Missing cops, missing father. Someone's going to put a rush on it, and it'll be my ass if there are any more roadblocks. I can call it all off before they arrive for whatever random reason. Maybe I'll look like an idiot, but whatever. Once they get here, I can't keep them out. Not even for a while."

"So less than twenty-four hours, and we need to find the missing people or destroy the Magister. Or both."

"Ideally both. If it's not too much trouble," Ventura suggested.

"We might have another problem," Herbert said, interrupting the conversation.

The ghost had left Shane and Ventura and walked several paces down the road closer to Burkitt.

"What's wrong?" Shane asked.

"Him," Herbert replied, pointing to the woods. A figure cloaked in darkness stood in the trees watching them.

"These guys never quit," Shane said, flexing his fingers. "Let's try this again."

CHAPTER 18

THE MAGISTER

The ghost stepped from the trees. He was older than any of them, perhaps in his sixties, with brown hair cropped short, and a face that looked prematurely aged, the way a farmer's face gets deeper lines from working in the sun. He was pale, though, and his mouth was curved into the hint of a smile.

He wore old boots that looked to be soft leather, faded around the edges and toes. His pants were dark, and he wore a linen shirt under a waistcoat. Everything looked exceedingly old and gave Shane pause. This was not a ghost who had died on a road trip through town or one of the citizens who perished in the sixties or seventies. This spirit went back much further.

"Who are you?" Shane asked.

The man's smile broadened. He looked so simple and forgettable. If he were in modern clothes, he would be lost in a crowd in moments. But his brown eyes had a sternness to them, and it grew in intensity as the man stopped on the road and raised his right hand.

Wind came up the path like a hurricane. Herbert remained unaffected but Shane nearly lost his footing. The blast hit him like a truck, and he braced himself, head down and arms up to protect his face.

Ventura was caught off-guard and swept backward. He skidded across the road and rolled several times before he stopped himself, face-down and laid flat. He shouted something Shane could not make out.

The temperature dropped and then kept dropping. The flesh on his forearms burned, and the wind cut through his clothing like he wore none.

Shane gritted his teeth and growled, turning toward the forest. The wind was unrelenting. It threatened to take him off his feet with each step. He was forced to crouch as he scrambled, almost crawling, toward the trees. Farther away, Ventura was crawling, making his way for the trees just as Shane had.

The temperature continued to drop like an onslaught of a winter storm, the worst Arctic winds, and then some. Shane took cover behind the trunk of a thick maple, shielding himself from the worst of the wind but not the intense cold. He watched as the branches and leaves froze and began to snap off.

Wood cracked and burst in the sudden shift in temperature. The liquids in the wood expanded rapidly as they turned to ice, forcing branches to explode and shatter into shards and dust.

Leaves fell to the road and shattered like glass. All Shane could do was hold his position behind the tree, away from the worst of it. He covered his head with his hands and waited. He had never experienced such a deep cold. If he had stayed on the road, he would have died.

"I have heard your name is Shane Ryan."

The accent was British. Shane lifted his head, and the ghost was crouched in front of him, smiling as the fierce wind continued to freeze the forest.

"The Magister?" Shane replied.

"Just Magister," the ghost answered. "What a unique creature you are. I should like to invite you to my home. Do you accept?"

Shane stared into the ghost's eyes. There was nothing there that looked malicious. He was so ordinary.

"Can't resist a personal invitation," Shane answered.

Magister smiled, and his teeth were slightly crooked, the most notable thing about his appearance.

"I trust you know where it is."

"Center of town," Shane confirmed.

"Very good. You will be most welcome. Do come quickly, lad. Bring your friends."

He rose, stepped into the blasting deep freeze, and then vanished. The wind died down soon after, and Shane got to his feet.

"Ventura?" he shouted. "Herbert?"

"Here," Herbert said, appearing on the road, a bewildered look on his face.

"Ventura?" Shane shouted again.

"Yeah. Jesus… yeah," came the reply from about a yard away behind another tree. He stumbled out, dirty and disheveled, cradling his left hand. "Think I got frostbite."

"That was him," Herbert said. "That was the Magister."

Ventura swore and joined them, blowing warm air on his hand as he held it close.

"You think you can defeat that guy in twenty-four hours?"

Shane grunted and reached into his jacket to find a cigarette. Magister had appeared to show off and nothing more. To his credit, it had been a good show. A casual display of deadly force was hard to ignore.

He lit the cigarette and took a long inhale. The fight might have to go a bit harder than usual, but he wasn't willing to give up just yet.

"You're not going with us anymore?" Shane asked.

Ventura grinned and slipped his hands into the gloves he'd brought, wincing as the frostbitten edge of his knuckles grated against the leather. He took off his suit jacket and tossed it to the side of the road, exposing the ironclad armor vest he'd made.

"Are you kidding? I'm absolutely going."

"I wouldn't," Herbert said. "If I were alive, I mean. That's a very powerful spirit."

"Strong ones are often overconfident. Especially old ones. Haven't been challenged in forever and don't think things through," Shane explained.

"Do we have a plan though?" Herbert asked.

Shane took the cigarette from between his lips and started walking back toward the house in the middle of town.

"We'll think of something."

They had no element of surprise, few weapons to speak of, and Herbert was not wrong. Magister was incredibly powerful. But all of that just made them underdogs.

Shane was in no rush, so they walked the remainder of the way down the hill and back to the corner that branched out to the scrapyard. The town of Burkitt was no longer as it had been when they left, however.

The sidewalks bustled with townspeople, pedestrians coming and going about their business. They walked dogs and chatted and shopped. People carried bags and couples held hands.

The diner was lit up with a big sign, and through the window, Shane could see families eating meals while they talked and laughed. People nodded and smiled and said hello as Shane and his companions walked past. The illusion was in full effect.

None of the ghosts were ghoulish in appearance. Everyone was as charming and happy as could be.

"This seems odd," Ventura said.

"All fake," Shane told him. "This is what the people who stop here see. This is why they stop. Why they get out of their cars."

"I'd never know the difference," Ventura said.

"I imagine no one does until it's too late," Shane agreed. They kept walking down the road toward the tree that blocked cars from going any farther. Even the tree was covered by the illusion. Instead of a dull, lifeless thing, it was green and full and looked like something people might gather under for a picnic.

"Welcome to Burkitt," passersby said as they continued forward. They smiled and nodded and gestured as though inviting the living to come on in.

"Come this way," an older woman said, inviting Shane onto the sidewalk alongside her.

"Come with me, young man. We'll take care of you," another man said, trying to take Ventura to the other side of the street. Shane ignored them and kept walking, and Ventura did the same.

They passed the tree, and the locals became more insistent.

"This way, please," a young woman said, flashing a smile at Ventura. A man reached for Shane's hand, and he pulled away, glaring at the ghost until it retreated.

The trees were tall and grew together above the street, creating a shadowy canopy that made the road darker as they walked.

"Come with me," a ghost demanded of Ventura. They tried to reach for him as well but held back, fearful of touching the vest he wore.

"Come," more of them said.

Those they had left behind near the diner were coming toward them now, at least a dozen, and more up ahead were leaving the sidewalks. The ghosts crowded around, encircling Shane and the others. They maintained the illusion, everyone looking pleasant and alive, but they reached out now, trying to grab and pull, all insisting the men join them.

"That's enough, everyone," a police officer shouted, dispersing the crowd as he approached from deeper in the town. "What are you lot trying to pull here?"

He approached Shane and Ventura with a hand resting on the butt of the gun at his side.

"You gentlemen need to come with me," the officer said.

"I think we're fine," Shane told him, not bothering to stop. The ghost pulled his sidearm and cocked the hammer.

"You're coming with me," the officer said firmly. "We don't need strangers just wandering the streets in Burkitt."

Shane puffed on his cigarette and squinted at the gun in the man's hands. It wasn't often he had a ghost firearm pointed at him.

"This guy's FBI. He outranks you," Shane said, gesturing to Ventura.

"Uh. That's true," Ventura said, not sure how to handle the situation. "At ease, officer."

Shane chuckled as the cop turned his gun on Ventura.

"Come with me. Now."

He pushed the gun close to Ventura's face. The agent looked at it closely and then raised one of his gloved hands. He pushed a leather-clad finger toward it, and it passed right through the barrel of the weapon until he reached the first iron stud.

Like flames spreading across spilled gasoline, Ventura's actions triggered a collapse in the display. The officer vanished, and the illusion under his feet died as well. It moved forward and out, across the street, and through the buildings and people.

The pedestrians vanished, and the sidewalks grew dull and cracked. Buildings fell into disrepair and the diner became a gutted, empty shell of a building once more. Every lie fell away, and the truth revealed itself. The dead town of Burkitt was on display once more.

The ghosts remained around them but no longer looked like the charming, happy populace of Burkitt. Some scuttled away as the illusion fell, but others remained. They were scarred and beaten and broken. Only a scant few looked like they could hope to pass for the living.

The windows of the ruined homes were full of faces. Eyes watched from every shadowy place. There was not a spirit in Burkitt that didn't know they were there.

"Oh…" Ventura said. He had never seen so many spirits in one place at one time. Shane was hard-pressed to think of more than a handful of times when he'd seen so many himself, not that he was counting. It was a lot for someone new to that world, but Ventura was holding up well.

"One ghost, a hundred ghosts, it's all the same," Shane assured him. Ventura scoffed.

"It's not remotely the same. What does that even mean? That's like comparing one stab wound to a hundred."

Shane shrugged. "Just means you don't need to act any differently. Not now. We've got somewhere to go."

"Easy for you to say," Ventura muttered.

Shane took another long drag on his cigarette and looked around at the assembled spirits. There were dozens, probably more than a hundred. It was as good an opportunity as any. The best he was going to get, given the constraints of the moment.

"Alright, everyone," Shane shouted, turning in a circle to look at the dead faces looking back at him. "I've got a deal for you."

CHAPTER 19

PLAN B

"What are you doing?" Herbert asked.

Shane held up his hands and waved them, ensuring he was getting the attention of all the dead.

"I had an idea," Shane answered quietly for just Herbert and Ventura to hear.

"The Custodian is gone; you probably know that by now. I just came here for him," Shane shouted. The surrounding ghosts did not approach, but they were listening.

"I destroyed the Custodian. I destroyed the Hunter. I would have left then if not for Magister. He wants me here. He's forcing me to keep destroying those of you he sends after me. And if you're okay with that, well, we can do something about it in a minute. But I'm going to destroy Magister before I leave."

"Is this a good idea?" Ventura whispered. Shane ignored him.

"So, you can stand by Magister, and against me, and see what happens. Or you can step aside and maybe spend the rest of your years in peace. You choose."

He put the cigarette back in his mouth and watched the houses that lined the street. Some of the spirits stirred, slipping away in darkness. Some, but not all. Not by far.

"Appealing to their better nature?" Ventura asked.

"Something like that. Heard not everyone in town is happy to be a lackey."

More ghosts faded away, but the number that remained was still high.

There were too many between them and Magister's house.

Shane wasn't certain they would get to the house unharmed. But even if they did and the ghosts followed, getting out again would be much harder. Even if he destroyed Magister, if too many were loyal, escape would still be nearly impossible. They were on everyone's radar now. There was no chance of sneaking past anyone.

"We can't get past all of them," Shane said, sizing up their odds.

"What?" Ventura said. "You said one or a hundred. You said it was the same."

"That was a minute ago. I think we need to do something else. This is just a trap, anyway. No need to play into his hands."

"Of course, it's a trap. The man invited us to his house," Ventura said.

Shane grinned and clapped the other man on the shoulder.

"Come on. I need you to meet someone."

Shane pinched out the butt of the cigarette and turned his back on Magister's house. If he stayed in the town limits, he felt like he might have a chance to stall. The ghost was probably used to people trying to hide or run. It sounded like that was part of the process. Shane would give him what he wanted, at least for a short time.

He led them back the way they had come and down some side streets they hadn't traveled before, guessing where he needed to go. Few of the ghosts from the main street followed, and those that did seemed only to be observing.

"Where are we headed?" Herbert asked as they zigzagged through unfamiliar streets.

"There," Shane said, pointing to a sign in the distance that rose over the rooftops.

"The scrapyard?"

"Magister's got some tricks; I think we need a couple, too."

They made their way to the front of the scrapyard once more and then inside. Lucky was not hidden in the swamp this time. Instead, the broken ghost was right where they had left him, near the camper, with his head sagging to one side.

"You found the dad but lost the kids and the wife?" the ghost asked, indicating Ventura.

"No, he's new here," Shane said. "I need help to pull some things together."

"What things?" the ghost asked.

"Iron things. And a truck that still runs."

Lucky had been in the scrapyard for more than half a century and had a good grasp of everything the place had in stock, even the new vehicles that had been brought in. There was not a lot of pure iron in modern vehicles, but there was some in older cars. Brake discs, crankshafts, and some engine parts would have been made of iron, and the scrapyard had plenty of old vehicles on hand.

"Go with Herbert. Find what you can," Shane told Ventura. Ghosts would be useless for moving any of it, but they could still find it and keep watch.

"I need you to find me something big," Shane told Lucky.

"Big, how?"

"Big and driveable. Rest is up to you," he said.

"I'll see what I have," the ghost replied before shambling away on unsteady legs.

Once he was alone, Shane started hunting through trunks. None of the vehicles had been looted; they had no reason to be. He found a couple of jerry cans after searching just a handful of vehicles.

He headed back to the front of the lot and took a length of hose he'd noticed on the way in the first time, cutting it to size on a random piece of rusty scrap before heading back to the vehicles. He could hear Ventura and Herbert talking in the distance but ignored them as he made his way to Jason's family's SUV.

Tools clanged as Ventura set to work on something. Shane used the hose to siphon gas from the SUV tank, spitting out a mouthful as it filled his mouth before he filled one of the red cans he'd found.

He'd filled three cans by the time he'd drained the two police cruisers. It was the freshest gasoline in the lot. As long as Lucky could find something to put it in.

"Lucky, what have you got?" Shane shouted.

"Come see," the ghost yelled back over the banging from Ventura.

Shane followed the sound of the ghost's voice around a barrier of stacked and rusted trash to the edge of the car swamp. The ghost stood next to a hulking green and white garbage truck.

"Big enough?" the ghost asked.

"Does it run?"

"Someone picked off the driver a month ago. No reason to assume the truck's not good if you need something driveable. Gotta warn you though, I think it's crap for speed."

"I don't need speed, Lucky. I need strength."

"Oh. Well. Have at it."

"Herbert!" Shane shouted. "Ventura!"

He walked around the truck, giving it a quick once-over to inspect the wheels and the exterior for any wear or damage, but it all seemed to be in as good condition as he could hope a garbage truck to be. He reached the gas cap, unscrewed it, and began to pour in his siphoned supply.

"We're stealing this?" Ventura asked as he approached with Herbert. His hands and face were smudged with grease from the work he'd been doing.

"Requisitioning," Shane corrected. "You found any iron?"

"Brake backing plates and a few random bits in an old engine that I just tore apart. Are we making weapons?"

"Armor." Shane patted the side of the truck. "As much as we can find, as quickly as we can find it."

"Oh, you need iron for the ghosts?" Lucky said then, finally catching on to the plan. "I got pure iron. Follow me."

The ghost led them away from the cars and to the far side of the scrapyard, near the oldest piles of junk. Almost everything was fuzzy and orange with rust, but the ghost passed it all until he came to a giant shipping container-sized dumpster underneath a rusted hulk of an industrial magnet.

"Back when this place was still in operation, I used to sort, separate, and sell everything. This is iron," he said, banging on the side of the container. Shane climbed up the wall and looked inside. The entire surface was a layer of thick orange corrosion. He grabbed a length of pipe and used it to poke through the furry cover, digging underneath to where the scrap was not nearly so rusted out.

The bin was full of everything from nails to pipes to shavings and decorative garden pieces. Some of it was crushed and bent, and some seemed perfectly fine other than the rust.

"There," Shane said, climbing carefully into the bin and trudging across.

It felt like an unsteady pebble beach under his feet, but he crossed the bin to pull out a stack of iron grilling pans. He held them up as Ventura climbed up to see what he was doing.

"That'll work," the agent said. "And those," he added, pointing out other pieces in relatively good condition.

"And these," Shane added, lifting some halved sections of cast iron pipe. He held one up and grunted. It would do.

The sun was heading toward the trees by the time Shane was satisfied with the scraps they'd collected. It wouldn't stand up to heavy gunfire or IEDs on the side of the road, but it would do against an army of surprised spirits who didn't know what they were getting into.

Both the cab and the front end of the garbage truck were wrapped in duct tape purloined from other stolen vehicles and covered as thoroughly as they could be in chunks of iron. The outside of the tires were coated in iron shavings mixed with an adhesive Lucky had found in another truck some years earlier. It was ugly as sin, and no ghost would get past it without an invitation.

Herbert opted to stay atop the back of the truck, away from the iron, on the lookout for any ghosts clever enough to reach that point. Shane and Ventura shared the cab, which was still stained with the blood of whoever had previously driven it.

"You really plan on storming the castle, huh?" Lucky asked when the truck was ready to go.

"Build a siege weapon to lay siege," Ventura said.

The ghost looked like he might have shrugged.

"Well, best of luck, I guess. This is… crazy. You seem crazy."

"Fun, isn't it?" Shane asked.

"I wouldn't say that. But, like I said, best of luck."

The keys to the truck were still in the ignition. Shane started the engine, and it roared to life, shaking the iron plates, and causing them to rattle profusely.

"He's right, you know. This is madness," Ventura said from the passenger seat.

"You want out?" Shane asked.

"No." The agent laughed. "I'm not going to have a chance to do anything like this for the rest of my life."

"Hell, you might die," Shane said with a laugh. He pulled another cigarette from his pack. It was his last one, which he decided to take as a good omen. It meant he'd need to get to a store soon and buy more. Which then meant they'd be done with Burkitt soon.

"You ready, Herbert?" he yelled, banging on the ceiling of the cab.

"Ready," the ghost yelled back.

"Before we go, I need you to hold this for me," Shane said, pulling the small, cloth-wrapped package from his pocket and handing it to the other man.

"What is it?" Ventura asked, folding back the cloth to expose a cameo necklace. He picked it up with two fingers and gasped, dropping it again. "Isn't this Herbert's?"

"Yep," Shane said.

"Why?"

"In case we get split up or something. That'll keep him with you. Just don't lose it."

"Huh," Ventura mumbled. He shrugged and slipped it into his pocket.

Shane put the truck in gear and backed up, knocking over piles of scrap as he did so. Instead of driving toward the front entrance, he headed to the fence they'd followed on the way in and drove through, crossing the rough terrain of yards until he rolled out onto a quiet street.

The truck shook and rattled loudly. Once they were on a flat road, Shane hit the gas and pushed the truck as much as he dared.

Ghosts watched from houses. Some crept out onto lawns and even on the sidewalks. Shane only caught glimpses of them as he maneuvered the vehicle through the zigzag of streets to get back to the main road to Magister's house.

"This is a quick and dirty plan, huh?" Ventura said.

"You gathered that," Shane replied.

"Have you ever done anything like this?"

"Attack a haunted house with a garbage truck? Never," Shane said, taking a long inhale from his cigarette. He turned onto Burkitt's main street and aimed the truck toward the end of the line. The large, old house on the hill, Magister's house, was the only thing in their path.

To the left and right, all the ghosts who had not left when he gave his warning surged out of the shadows.

"You ready?" Shane said, shifting gears.

"God no," Ventura replied. "Hit it."

Shane pushed his foot down on the gas.

CHAPTER 20

MASTER OF CHAOS

The garbage truck roared, and the iron plates rumbled in their duct tape lashings. Ghosts burst from all corners in a rush. They ran and crawled and leaped from windows and shadows and dark corners.

Shane gritted his teeth around his cigarette and held the wheel steady. The spirit of a young man missing half of his face stood in the road as though he might convince Shane to stop or swerve. The front of the vehicle was strapped with cast-iron grates and a large, wrought-iron fence piece set up like a cattle catcher. Shane plowed straight through the ghost, watching him blink from existence as the iron did its job.

More came at the sides of the vehicle, targeting Shane and Ventura in the cabin. They bounced off cast iron cooking surfaces, brake backings, and pipe segments. They all vanished in a blink, thrust back to the house or wherever their haunted items were stored. Wherever kept them out of Shane's way long enough to get where he was going.

Magister's house grew closer. In the failing light of day, Shane could see the deflected spirits returning, swarming over the house like wasps in their nest. Each one that bounced off the truck became a defender of the house.

"Drop 'em," Shane said.

Ventura pulled on one of the central levers set into a dashboard control panel. Hydraulics in the truck whirred to life, and the forks used to pick up dumpsters began to lower over the top of the truck to the front.

"Everything good?" Shane shouted out the window to Herbert. The ghost said something in reply, lost over the sound of the truck.

The truck reached the base of the hill and started up, tires tearing through the soil and grass. Ventura held onto the door and placed his other hand on the ceiling to stabilize himself as the forks settled into place.

Ghosts jumped from the house toward the truck, bouncing off the iron armor again and being forced to start over. Soon, there was nothing but the house in Shane's field of vision. He kept his foot on the gas.

The forks smashed through the side wall of the house. Shane lurched in his seat but held the wheel, and the truck barely slowed. The front end smashed into dark wood and the truck crashed into the building, sending wooden shards everywhere.

The windshield cracked. Shane could see nothing at all. He kept his foot on the gas. The sound of the collapsing house, the roaring engine, and the rattling iron was like the end of the world.

Light filled the cracked glass once more, the last light of day, and Shane slowed the truck to a stop as they cleared the far wall. The house crumbled to ruins behind them, crashing down onto the truck and across the hill in all directions.

The gears struggled as Shane put the vehicle in park and pulled off his seat belt.

"You alive?" he said to Ventura.

"More than I expected to be," the agent replied. He secured the iron-studded gloves on his hands and pulled a length of old, rusty chain from the floor between his feet. "Let's go."

The men left the vehicle, surveying the damage they had left in their wake. The house, ancient as it was, had collapsed entirely. The second floor must have broken apart on the way down. Only the wall closest to the swamp remained, holding up nothing at all. Everything else was scattered across the hill like a bomb had gone off.

Herbert had already left the roof of the truck.

"I've got the cellar," he shouted, vanishing into the destruction.

They had assumed that the cellar the boy had told them about was set into the earth and would remain even if the house was destroyed. Herbert could slip inside the easiest. Shane and Ventura remained above to fight the spirits and take on Magister until Herbert found the father, if he was there at all.

Ghosts swarmed out of the damage. Ventura, clad in iron, wielded a pair of bars like they were knives, beating at anything that came close. He used the chain to swing at those farther away, the end wrapped around his wrist so he could lash out at a moment's notice and catch anything in range.

Ventura joined Shane at the rear of the truck, as close to the ruined house as they could get without stumbling through the unsafe wreckage. It was not ideal grounds on which to fight, and they had no advantage in terms of cover. Certainly not in terms of numbers. But they had thrown their enemy off, and that was a good start. That and their defenses.

Shane had fixed half segments of cast iron pipes he had found to his forearms, taping them below the elbow and at his wrist, creating a somewhat ungainly, poor man's version of medieval vambraces. His arms would get tired a little faster than normal, but it ensured nothing would be able to restrain his arms below the elbow. And it made his backhands that much more dangerous.

Ventura took up a defensive position, nervous though he was. Ghosts approached and failed to touch him time and again, moving too hastily to plan an attack that might get past his armor. Shane focused on the more cautious few that managed to get around him.

The first spirit to make it past Ventura to Shane was that of a woman, middle-aged with a round face that was missing most of the flesh. Her wounds bled openly across the plain, gray dress she wore.

She had crept around behind the men and moved to attack Shane from behind. He saw her long before she was in range and sidestepped the attack, kicking her leg out from under her as she did so, causing her to collapse.

Not a single word was exchanged. The numbers were not in favor of the living, and Shane did not have time to waste. He took the ghost by the back of the head and slammed his fist down hard, then continued pressing until he felt it give.

The ghost's body burst violently, and he was knocked backward, where a second spirit jumped on him to capitalize. He lashed out quickly and slammed the cast-iron pipe into the ghost's gut. It vanished and allowed him to gain his footing before a third approached, followed by a fourth.

Ventura cried out as a ghost managed to slip close enough to slice open the back of his leg. Shane destroyed a second spirit and came to the other man's side, using the iron to force back others.

"You alright?" he asked.

"It's fine. Not deep," Ventura answered. The amount of blood on his leg said differently, but he was still standing.

They needed word from Herbert, some sign that he either found the man or that there was no man to find. But the big ghost had not returned.

"The entrance is there," Shane said, pointing across the wreckage to trapdoors that were set into the ground.

The men made their way around the rubble, fighting off the ghosts that continued to rush at them. Coming in numbers was not working, and the spirits soon learned this. Most held back now, covering the wreckage of the house like cockroaches, simply watching as others moved in smaller groups to find a way past the iron defenses.

Those that were deflected by iron were back in seconds. The haunted items had to be somewhere in the destroyed house or the cellar, just as Shane had been told. There was no rest period between their vanishing and returning to fight.

Shane knew they would never defeat so many of the dead, and he had no intention of trying. But there was a difference between not defeating them and not losing. The ghosts could do nothing to overcome the effect of iron.

"They're slowing down," Ventura noted as they passed the still-standing wall at the rear of the house. The ghosts followed them, like a pack of wolves stalking prey. They kept in range and kept close watch, but few tested the limits now. Few dared to get close.

It was not just iron that kept them at bay. They had seen Shane destroy two of their kind. They now knew the story about the Custodian was true.

Shane could see the reluctance. Lucky had not lied to him. Not all the ghosts wanted to fight for Magister. And, given an excuse not to, they were avoiding it. They still looked like his loyal troops, but they were not rushing in to find weak points in Shane and Ventura's defenses. They didn't want to risk it.

"Some ghosts are smarter than they look," Shane said.

He cared little for the rabble that had assembled. Magister was not among them. He was somewhere else still, which meant he was still playing a game. He still had a plan. That was what worried Shane.

The two men approached the entrance that led down to the cellar slowly. A ghost sat atop the doors, while others were arranged around a defensive line. It would be hard to get past them if they all held fast. Using iron would be easy enough, but they would reappear almost immediately. It was not a matter of whether they could defend the cellar doors, but if they would.

"This will go a lot more smoothly if you guys just back off," Shane suggested, looking from ghost to ghost.

Some looked to have died a hundred years in the past; some looked like they were from only a year or two ago. Some had been killed brutally, their bodies destroyed; others bore almost no signs of trauma.

Shane did not know what bound some of the ghosts to Magister and made others reluctant. There did not seem to be much rhyme or reason. It was something he was not meant to see. Something happened when death and life fractured, and the ghosts let go of who they once were.

The spirit on the doors moved forward. It was a man, younger than

Shane, and shorter. The top of his head was missing, and the inside of his skull was visible. His eyes didn't blink, and a constant stream of blood flowed from his nose.

"He's going to torture you for weeks," the ghost said. There was no emotion in his voice; no anger or hate. It didn't even sound like it was meant to intimidate.

"That'll give me time to catch up on some sleep," Shane replied.

The ghost frowned and reached for Shane's neck.

"Don't resist. It's better this way."

Shane sighed and pushed the ghost's hand aside. The others moved as one and Ventura beat them back with the iron bars while Shane closed the small gap between himself and the scalped ghost.

"This makes it easier, you know," he told the ghost. He grasped the edges of the spirit's exposed skull in both hands and simply pulled in opposite directions. There was a snapping sound and the ghost's eyes rolled back as the skull split in two just before it burst.

Shane stumbled back under the force of the explosion but maintained his footing. The other ghosts backed off, retreating to the crowd of others in the ruined house.

The sun had set, and Burkitt was fully dark now, save for the light of a half moon in a partially cloudy sky that was still mostly hidden beyond trees. Only the lights of the still-running garbage truck allowed them to see the top of the hill. The doors to the cellar were clear.

"Go," Ventura said, holding the iron bars at the ready. "I'll cover your back."

Shane opened the cellar.

CHAPTER 21
THE LION'S DEN

Cold air rushed out and hit Shane in the face. The doors fell to the sides of the stone steps that led down into the earth, landing with a loud slam. The truck idled in the background, a steady hum that provided the only other sound in the world.

Magister smiled. He stood on the landing at the bottom of the stone steps, looking up at Shane.

"I am so glad you could make it," the ghost said.

The freezing wind that rose from behind Magister was like a freight train. There was no warning this time and no place to hide. The wind struck Shane and sent him flying backward toward the road. It was like being hit by a glacier, a deep freeze that resonated through his body. He gasped involuntarily as every muscle spasmed and contracted as one, his body so desperate to flee the sudden chill that he felt everything pull close and tight as he sailed through the air.

The painful sting was everywhere, but he felt it most in his eyes and nose. It had been only an instant, the barest of breaths, but the cold froze the surface of his eyes and the mucous membranes inside his skull. The pain was unbearable.

He fell in a heap at the base of the hill, unaware of where he was or how long he had been falling. The blast was so disorienting, he hadn't even thought to try to move or brace his fall.

To his left, Ventura suffered the same fate. The FBI agent rolled down the hill as though he were dead, only making sounds when he came to a full stop. Even then, they were only pained gasps as he caught his breath.

He struggled to right himself, to get to his hands and knees, but failed and fell face-first into the dirt.

"Ventura," Shane croaked. His throat felt like he had swallowed razor blades, and his words were a quiet garble.

The cold settled into his skull, and the pain bore into his brain. Shane held his head in his hands, trying to will it away and regain his senses as something took hold of his ankle.

He swore and swiped blindly with his hand. He felt something bat his arm away and realized the tape on his wrists had come loose. The iron cuffs he'd made were gone, lost in the fall.

Shane rolled his thumbs across his fingers. The iron rings were missing. He cursed and looked up as he was dragged up the hill by a small, frail-looking spirit.

He kicked out with his free foot and clipped the ghost in the back of the leg, causing it to stumble. They were halfway up the hill, halfway toward the open cellar door.

"Accept it. It's easier this way," the ghost said, turning on him and reaching for his ankle again. He kicked it square in the face this time, heel to nose, and the spirit reeled back, clutching its face.

Another ghost leaped on him then, rolling him face-down and holding his face into the dirt.

"It's easier," the new ghost repeated. Shane reached back and grabbed the ghost's wrist, twisting it awkwardly until something snapped.

The spirit cried out and Shane sat up. Another cold hand took him by the ankle, then both ankles, and yanked him forward so he fell face-first once more.

Shane tried to grab hold of something, to sink his fingers into the soil and slow the dragging, but more cold hands took his wrists and peeled his arms away from the ground. Soon he was being carried, a ghost on each limb, back toward Magister.

"Shane!"

Ventura was on his feet. One hand held the end of the chain at chest level while his other arm was up. The chain spun, creating a loud and ominous hum as it whirled above his head. He had used one of the stray pieces of duct tape from Shane's arm to secure one of his iron bars through the final link, creating a weapon like a flail.

The chain-and-bar weapon swung wildly, passing unobstructed through spirits that vanished the moment it touched them. Shane fell to the ground, no longer in the clutches of anything. He got to his knees, ready to bolt, and stopped.

"Your six," he yelled.

A pack of spirits had flanked Ventura and more crawled and slinked on the ground around him. His weapon was a threat, but they were coming in low from behind to take him out where he was not guarded.

Ventura turned, swinging the chain down through a swath of enemies. A fast-moving spirit ran at his back and pulled the edge of his vest, grabbing a section free of iron and tearing it away. The seams burst and the garment tore loose, hanging from one shoulder.

The agent swore and something else took hold of Shane. He struggled to roll over but was held down by more icy hands.

"Ventura, go," Shane yelled at him.

The FBI agent turned, spinning the chain-and-bar combo wildly. Another spirit pulled at his vest, nearly tearing it from his body. They made eye contact. Ventura shook his head, yelling wordlessly, the panic clear in his eyes as he swung for anything that moved.

Every time he turned his back, another made a play for his vest. It hung limply from his left shoulder now, folded over on itself and offering little protection. Only the chain kept the ghosts at bay, and he had to move fast to keep it that way.

"Leave!" Shane shouted.

His body was thrust backward. He sailed through the air, hurled back like a sandbag, and tumbled down the stone stairs. He heard Ventura yelling above, the sound growing fainter and more distant as he hit the bottom and rolled across the floor of the cellar.

The wooden doors slammed shut and Shane was plunged into darkness. He lay on the cold stone where Magister had once stood, his head spinning after hitting the hard surface.

He needed to get back outside. Ventura was useless without iron. He'd be killed in seconds. He had no natural defense against the ghosts.

Shane sat up. His head throbbed, and he couldn't stave off the dizziness. The only sounds in the cellar were the muffled sounds of the outside. The hum of the garbage truck was like white noise filling the void. He put his hand on the bottom step, feeling the cold stone, and moved to stand.

His head swam, and he stopped, giving himself another minute. Part of him wanted to rush up the steps and get back to Ventura, but that was not the plan. Ventura still had weapons. He had the chain. He could fix the vest. He could run like Shane had told him to. Shane needed to focus on why they went there to begin with.

The cellar was where he needed to be. He needed to find Herbert and Jason's father. And he needed to find Magister. All of them were down in the cellar. Or should have been.

Slowly, and painfully, Shane rose to his feet. He used the wall for support, to keep himself upright while he took deep breaths and let his head stop spinning. No ghosts had followed him down, and if Magister was still waiting, he was doing so coyly.

The darkness of the cellar was impenetrable. He couldn't see his hand in front of his face. Not enough had been visible when he looked in previously to give him an idea of even a general layout.

Shane listened for sounds of movement, sounds of whispers or scraping or anything. There was nothing beyond the sound of the truck.

"Well, you got me here. What now?" he asked the darkness.

No answer came from Magister or any other spirit. Shane waited as seconds passed and then grunted. Magister liked to torture and draw things out. This was probably all in his wheelhouse. But something would happen before long. Shane decided to push up the timetable.

He reached into his jacket and pulled out the Zippo, striking the wheel and setting it aflame. The light did not spread far, but it was enough to find his way. Shane held it out in front of him and stepped away from the stairs.

The cellar was made from cobblestones and a sandy white mortar. Up on the hill as it was, it was free from the moisture of the swamp and looked like it had been relatively dry for probably the better part of two hundred years. Everything was dusty and white and reminded Shane of old bones.

The space before him was large and open, save for the random pillars that held up the ceiling. They were made of the same stone and mortar but had been built to include cubbies for storage. The nearest held an ancient lantern, still half full of oil.

"Well, look at that. Convenient." Shane took the dusty lantern from the stone shelf and blew on it. He wiped away some cobwebs and opened the small, glass door, pushing the Zippo in against the old, blackened wick.

The flame took hold dully, producing a thick, black smoke that rose in a wispy, weedy tendril through the vent. Shane tried to adjust the small wheel on the side, but that only succeeded in making more smoke. The light was dim and the flame paltry, but it would do. He closed the door to protect the flame and slipped the lighter back into his pocket.

Two more steps and something clattered underfoot. Shane lowered the lamp and stepped back from a pair of rusty shackles. The chain, in better condition than Ventura's, was attached to the same pillar as the lantern had been, held with a thick iron ring pinned into the stone.

He walked around the room, discovering more shackles on each pillar, but nothing else in the storage holes and nobody locked in the shackles. There were at least a dozen sets. A dozen people who could have been imprisoned in the basement at any point.

Shane found the wall and more shackles, attached so high up that people would have had to be restrained with their hands above their heads. The dim light showed stains on the wall, old blood and scratches, and gouges in some places, though it was hard to say what tool or weapon had made them.

He walked the wall in shadows, letting the flickering, deep yellow light show what it could until he came to the next set of shackles. These were not empty.

The body was not old. Held with wrists above its head, it was slumped so that its knees bent but could not touch the ground. Shane had to get closer to tell that it had been a man. There was not a strip of flesh left on the body. Every inch of it had been peeled away.

The floor was bloody, but not nearly bloody enough. If the man had been flayed on the wall, someone had done a good job of cleaning up. There were bloody footprints, and some splatters, but nothing more.

Everything glistened in the dim lantern light. Shane reached out and touched the man's arm. It was cold and tacky to the touch. He had not even had time to dry yet.

Without flesh, Shane could only guess what the man's face once looked like. But it was not far-fetched to assume this was Jason's father. A fresh kill, maybe done in haste or to teach a lesson. Lucky had assured Shane that Magister liked to draw out his kills, but maybe this was an exception. Or just a cruel reminder of who had the power.

Shane lowered the lantern to his side. If the goal was to intimidate him, it was having the opposite effect.

He wanted to destroy Magister more than ever.

Chapter 22
Dark Places

Shane found nothing else in the room, but several doors led to other chambers, and those branched into even more. The first such room he discovered was even dustier than the room with the body.

The room housed wooden shelves set into the walls. Each shelf had old clay pots or glass jars and bottles. Some were sealed with wax; others were empty. Some of the bottles looked half-full of some dark liquid. Nothing was labeled, and everything was covered in thick dust.

The next room was the same. Small, wooden boxes, old clay pots, and more filled spaces and empty spots on the floor. Shane kicked one of the clay pots, shattering it. The pieces fell apart to reveal the bleached bones of a human hand kept within, fragments now and no longer connected as a whole appendage.

Shane used the toe of his boot to move the pieces and get a clearer look at the hand. It had been cut off, the bones at the wrist showing signs of something sharp having been used. He leaned down slowly and touched one of the finger bones. He expected a surge of cold, some indication that what he was feeling was a haunted item, but there was nothing. It was just a regular, severed hand, if such a thing could ever be considered regular.

He knocked bottles from a shelf, inspecting the remains with the lamp and discovering shattered teeth in one and a warped golden earring in another. The next pot he broke contained a watch with a broken face. The one after that held pieces of a skull.

Everything looked like they should have been haunted items. He'd encountered enough to know what sort of things held spirits to the world.

But none of them were. None had that chill, that feeling that there was a spirit bound to them.

For all the bottles and jars he passed, it looked like there could have been enough for every ghost in Burkitt. It was a collection to shame even James Moran's. He wondered how many rooms there were. But if they were not haunted items, it made no sense.

Unless, he thought, *they weren't always like this.*

The items he'd seen were all broken or warped. Lucky had told him that Magister sometimes fed on the other spirits. Maybe the storage rooms were shrines that held the mangled remains of what were once haunted items, damaged after Magister stripped away the soul.

The door at the end of the storage room did not lead to another room full of items. Instead, he found a hallway, narrow and with a low ceiling made of the same cobblestones. It was long and curved, and Shane thought it might be circling the base of the hill below the house, but it was hard to tell. He already felt disoriented from the blow to the head he'd received earlier.

When he passed the first skeleton, he paused to inspect it. The body was older than the man in the first room had been. There was almost nothing left on the bones, just the stains of old tissue and some ragged bits of nearly petrified flesh.

Shane continued around the curve and discovered more skeletons. They were not shackled in place; they were just slumped here and there. They looked like people who had fallen and given up. Most were propped against the wall like they had died sitting up. He passed a dozen before coming upon a wooden door set into the stone.

The wood was stained nearly black and had a finish that reflected the light. There was no lock, only an old brass doorknob that was set very low for a person even of average height. Shane had to lean over to take hold of it.

He paused, his hand on the knob, and listened for any sounds. The brass was cool in his hand, but not suspiciously so. The hum of the garbage truck could not be heard anymore. There was just stillness. He turned the knob and pushed the door.

Light was the first thing to draw Shane's attention. The room was lit by thick, old candles set into wall sconces. A half-dozen lined walls to the left and right, each set atop a frozen cascade of ancient wax tendrils that reached the floor below them. The pools to either side had not been cleaned in a long while, maybe ever, the result being blobs of old wax that merged on the cobblestone in thick, white smears.

The room was a chapel of some kind. Narrow wooden pews, side by side, filled the center of the space ten deep. Shane wondered how anyone brought them down given the narrow dimensions of the hallway he'd just traveled.

The front of the room featured a dark wooden pulpit flanked by two narrow tables and mountains of what looked like trash on the tables and in the pews. Moonlight cascaded through the torn open ceiling, a hole that the garbage truck had ripped to leave it all exposed.

Nothing else was in the room. No decorations, symbols, or religious icons to indicate if it had been some kind of church or just a gathering place.

Shane walked up the center aisle. The piles of trash became clearer as he approached. Pocket watches. Silver dollars. Old glasses, a hairpin, a painting, a wedding ring. And bones. Many, many bones.

If the other room was the shrine to all the ghosts Magister had lost, the chapel was home to those who remained.

It looked like the plan had once been to arrange them neatly on the tables, but there grew to be too many. Similar items were piled together in some places, but it seemed like even that method of organization had been abandoned. Eventually, things were just dumped. Hundreds of items, hundreds of ghosts, all bound in this one room. In the heart of Magister's home.

Shane plucked a watch from the mass, a cheap old pocket watch from the forties that probably only had sentimental value to the owner at the time but would now fetch a few dollars as an antique. He held it in the light of the half moon. It felt like ice in his hand, and he dropped it.

They were all haunted. They were all there, under Magister's eye.

"Do you like it?"

Magister spoke from behind him. Shane turned and saw him in the doorway. Herbert was with him. The big ghost stood to one side, Magister's hand on his shoulder.

"This... collection?" Shane asked.

"Yes. My people. My town," Magister replied. "My legacy."

"Your army," Shane corrected. Magister smiled.

"If need be. A nation needs an army. You cannot be left defenseless in this world."

"So, you're a nation now?" Shane said. "Was a town just a second ago."

"It is both. And more. A nation. A family. An entire world. The world beyond your world. But you see it. You can touch it! Surely you would not deny that it is real."

"I don't deny that. But if you're getting at some sort of brave-new-world-of-ghosts with you as lord, then I'm going to stop you now."

Magister grinned wider and held out his arms.

"Lord? No. I'm Magister," he said.

"At the cost of how many dead?" Shane asked, pushing a pile of items off the table, causing them to clatter across the stone floor.

"Cost? This is not cost. This is reward. Allow me to demonstrate."

With one hand still on Herbert's shoulder, Magister reached out his other hand and grabbed the big ghost's arm. The motion was so swift that Shane didn't realize what was happening until it was too late. He pulled Herbert's arm from his body like tearing a petal from a flower and then cast it aside.

The arm tumbled through the air for only a moment before it fell apart into nothing. Herbert screamed in shock, looking at the shoulder joint where his arm had once been.

Shane dropped the lantern and ran at Magister. He made it only two steps before something fell on him from above.

Cold hands encircled his throat. Shane stumbled to one side, the sudden appearance of a ghost on his back surprising him. He fell to the ground between a pair of pews where he was able to get a grip on two of the fingers on his throat. He broke them off, and the ghost shrieked.

The spirit released him and cradled its hands while Shane got to his feet and tackled it. He had seen the ghost before, one of the few protecting the cellar doors.

No longer interested in Herbert, Magister focused on Shane as he fought. The ghost-lackey went for his neck again, and Shane smashed a fist into its nose, breaking it. A second punch broke its jaw. Shane's hands closed over the skull, a thumb sinking into the ghost's eye, and he slammed down with all the force he could muster.

The pews were knocked back, and the haunted items were scattered about. Shane lurched back under the force of the ghost's destruction as well, but he made a quick recovery, getting to his knees first and then his feet as he stared Magister down.

"Remarkable," the spirit said as though he had just watched a magic trick. "How do you do this?"

Shane's eyes darted from Magister to Herbert and back. Herbert took a slow, careful step away which Magister either didn't notice or didn't care about. He was focused on Shane now, which was exactly what Shane wanted.

"Why me specifically?" Shane asked. "Or just the mechanics of how I do it at all?"

"Mechanics... ah!" Magister said, relishing the word. He smiled and shrugged. "Both, I should say. I want to know how you came by this power and how it works. What is the nature of it? Can it be learned?"

Herbert backed away again, and Shane leaned against the pulpit.

"I don't think I can enlighten you as much as you might like. I can't say with any certainty why it works this way for me but not for others. I had what you might call a bad experience with one of your kind when I was younger."

"It tried to kill you?" Magister asked.

"Yes," Shane said with a nod. "Came very close."

"But you triumphed. You mastered this ability, this power to fight back. To fight against Death itself."

"Maybe not Death. Manifestation of death, certainly. Never met the real Death."

Magister grinned and offered up his hands, palms up, in a placating manner.

"Perhaps you have and did not realize it."

"You?" Shane said, smiling. "A killer is not Death any more than a frying pan is a chef."

Magister's laugh was deep and boisterous. He looked genuinely amused by Shane's quip.

"So it can be said," the ghost agreed. "But tell me, how does it work? Is it something you must trigger? Is it a process? Instinct?"

"None of the above," Shane explained. "It just *is*. All the time. To me, you are as solid and as vulnerable as any living being."

"Any living being," Magister repeated as Herbert backed right to the door. He turned his head to look at the big ghost then. "You may go, by the way."

Herbert froze in place and then looked from Magister to Shane, who nodded.

"Find Ventura. Get to safety," Shane said.

Herbert left without a word, and Magister turned back to face Shane once more.

"You were saying," the ghost said. That Shane had been stalling to let Herbert escape seemed to mean nothing to him.

"Not sure what else there is to tell."

"The process. The function and form of it all. Is it permanent? How does it feel for you? Does it cause pain to the spirit you dispatch?"

"Ah," Shane said. He wished he had a cigarette. He wasn't much for lectures, but anything that kept him alive was worth it.

"You want the details."

CHAPTER 23

THE DETAILS

"I don't know that the dead feel pain," Shane began. Magister cut him off right away, laughing again.

"Oh, but they do. They do, sir. Not the pain you feel, not the pain of blood and meat and bone. That is nothing but nominal pain. Fleetingly mortal. The dead feel the deepest pain. The pain of time. It never ends, you see. It is like water dripping on stone, wearing it down forever and ever. It has no mercy, no remorse. No sympathy."

"You feel time wearing on you?" Shane asked.

"Always. The dead do not eat. They do not sleep. They do not live. All they do is… that is all. They are. I am. Forever, sir. Forevermore. The only thing that is truly here with me is time. This place, you, this conversation, is but a mote of dust in an infinite river. Long from now, I will still be, and this will be but a memory of a memory. Me and time, dancing forever. Fighting forever. That is the pain of being dead."

"That's poetic," Shane said. He really wished he had a cigarette. "People would put that on crochet wall hangings."

"Is it permanent?" Magister asked again.

"Seems that way," Shane answered.

"And the dispatched spirit? The power, the energy that was the core of its being, what of that?"

Shane was not sure how to answer. He thought he understood what the ghost was talking about, but there was not much to say about it. Still, he needed to keep stringing the ghost along while he came up with a way to get the drop on him.

"It dissipates," Shane replied.

"I saw." The ghost gestured to the pews that were pushed aside by the exploding spirit. "Wasted, one might say. And what a waste for someone as unique as yourself."

"I'm fine with it," Shane said. If he could get on top of the pulpit, he could climb out through the ceiling, he thought. He could regroup with Ventura and Herbert, perhaps plan for a fight against Magister. There had to be something he could do.

"What if you could do more?" the ghost asked. Shane raised an eyebrow.

"Meaning?"

"You are a rare creature in this world, sir. A ghost killer. Who has ever heard of such a thing? I have not, and I have been here a very long time."

"I don't think I'm unique in what I do. Besides, you've been hidden away in the middle of nowhere," Shane pointed out.

Magister laughed and nodded.

"True. But do you see my vision, sir? I was once an explorer, you know. A pioneer in search of adventure. I built this house—the one you destroyed so quickly—with my own hands. I was alone here when this was nothing but a forest. I made this a home, and then an outpost, and finally a town. A community. And I am still building to this day."

"Your expansion," Shane added. Magister pointed at him, a fiery look in his eye.

"Expansion! Exactly. With time, you learn that all things are possible, including pushing beyond your boundaries. I need not be limited by the arbitrary borders of one place. Like you, I do the impossible. I will push Burkitt outward and consume the lands around us. Villages and towns and one day cities. They can all fall under the auspices of my rule."

"But you can't travel that far," Shane said.

"I need not. Does the King need to leave his throne to rule? He sends emissaries. He makes lords watch over the serfs and collect his taxes. I will be no different."

"Lords like the Custodian?" Shane asked.

Magister smiled, but it was grim.

"Yes. He was a rarity, too. And you got rid of him."

"He had it coming."

"A true leader cannot focus on losses but must plan for the next victory. I congratulate you on your defeat of the Custodian. It could not have come easily."

Shane nodded but had nothing more to say on the matter. Magister struck him as the sort of man who would sleep with a friend's wife and buy the guy a drink afterward. There was an ingrained smugness to the dead man. Maybe the arrogance of age, from having survived for so long. He was so sure of himself, and that confidence did not feel like it would waver.

"I can't imagine this conversation is just about making me feel good about myself," Shane said. "You want something."

He knew what Magister wanted. He knew before he even met him. But he was buying as much time as he could. Ventura and Herbert needed to get away, and hopefully, they had. All he needed to do was find a way to destroy Magister and follow. It sounded very easy in his head.

"Isn't it obvious?" Magister asked.

"It is," Shane agreed. The ghost smiled.

"You wish to hear a formal proposal. The terms of the agreement. That's good business. I want you, sir. I want you to be mine."

"You want me as your newest lord?"

"No, sir. You are far too valuable an asset for such a pittance. You should be a prince! How about I make you my right hand, in time."

The way he added the final words "in time" stuck in Shane's head. Magister was patient. Time was meaningless. He was talking about killing Shane and keeping him captive for years. Decades. Forever, even. That's what he wanted. Because he was convinced Shane's abilities would make him a unique ghost. Some one-of-a-kind monster like the Custodian.

"Burkitt only works with the right residents. Like an army made of rabble versus one made of elite soldiers, you can make a mundane thing better. I have had to settle… many times. I have settled on those that came back unimpressive or unremarkable. And some had to be sacrificed for the greater good. To make way for the Custodian. To make way for you. You can be a part of what is to come. Of my vision for Burkitt."

"Not interested," Shane said.

"No one is, at first," Magister acknowledged. "You don't know the vision, sir. You don't know the glory that I will one day create."

"I have an idea," Shane said.

He glanced up at the hole in the ceiling again, at the broken timbers and fractured bits. There was a bent support beam only a few paces away. It looked like it would hold his weight if he was fast. If he timed it right, he could scramble up and out. The truck was close; he could find iron with which to defend himself and keep the other ghosts at bay. He just needed to get close enough to Magister, but away from the cold he produced. If he could get hands on him, he could defeat him.

"Imagine the peace, sir. If my borders expand to the east, to the Atlantic shores and then west, across that frontier and into the wilderness, all the way to the Pacific. Imagine the serenity if every citizen of this nation is taken into the fold. If I can mold them and direct them to a place beyond mortal life. Picture it. Can you?"

"The murder of everyone in America? I'll give you credit for having a lofty goal. Do we get Canada and Mexico too, or is this only a patriotic endeavor?"

"It's not a joke, sir. Do you not see what I'm offering? You say murder, I say salvation. I have been here for hundreds of years. Where will you be in two centuries? Rotten? Old bones in a dusty box? Why should people suffer that fate when there is another way? I have the secret. I know the path!"

"The path to death," Shane clarified.

"To eternity! I push the flesh until it breaks. And then I push more. And the result is a new existence. A new life beyond death in which time no longer has hold. I can give this to the whole world! And you could be at my side maintaining order. My knight. My enforcer!"

Shane kept his expression measured. Magister was pushing extinction in a way he could have never imagined. Extinction as salvation and a new world made entirely of ghosts forged by his hand. Forged through torture to guarantee the birth of a ghost in the aftermath.

"So, you want to save the world from mortality by offering eternity. And you'd be in charge," Shane said.

"Your tone suggests you think me arrogant, but who else, sir? Someone needs to be the center, and I am the progenitor of this world. I am the source."

"The Alpha and the Omega?" Shane suggested.

"Certainly."

Shane nodded. There were Messiah complexes, and then there were Messiah complexes. He wondered what sort of person Magister had been before he died, back when he was the man living in the house up on the hill. Maybe that was what had driven him mad in the first place. Isolation and then years alone as a spirit pushed him over the edge.

"You still hold life as sacrosanct. I see it on your face," Magister continued. "But you, of all people, should have a greater perspective. You walk in my world and your own. You see the frailty of flesh. The weakness of life. Life is a precursor to what I offer. It is the pain you must endure before your eternal reward. These are not my ideas; this is how it has always been."

"If you're comparing Burkitt to Heaven, you've got a vastly different understanding from most people, I think," Shane told him.

Magister smiled softly, a paternal expression, and sighed dramatically.

"I do not blame you for being resistant. Everyone is at first. You cannot know a thing until you experience it. I have not the words to convince you, and I would not try. You will see for yourself, and when you know, then we will revisit our discussion. It will take time, and that is your first lesson. Taking time. You must take it until there is none left to give. Then, when you have abandoned time, you will be ready to see me again. I have great faith in you."

Magister relaxed then. The two remained still for a long moment, sizing each other up, when Shane finally took a step toward the broken beam in the ceiling.

"So, that's it then?" he asked, puzzled.

"It is, sir," Magister answered. "I will see you when you are ready."

"Then I can just leave?" Shane asked, pointing at the beam he planned to climb.

Magister smiled and shook his head.

"Of course not, sir. You will never leave this place again."

Chapter 24
TRAPPED

The cold snap hit as suddenly as it had before. The temperature drop was enough to make Shane gasp. Above him, ghosts crowded over the hole in the ceiling, blocking his path to any potential escape.

Shane ran at Magister. It was the only play he had. To destroy the ghost as quickly as he could and put an end to whatever long-winded and utterly insane plans the old ghost may have had for the future.

Freezing air blasted against Shane's body harder, a wind that came from nowhere but blew like a storm. He felt the cold searing into his flesh, pulling at him, and he struggled against it. Only a handful of steps separated him from Magister, but it was like fighting against a hurricane to move even an inch.

He held his arms before his head and kept his face turned, trying to shield himself from the terrible cold.

"Look how you fight," Magister shouted above the roaring wind. Shane could not see the ghost, but he could feel the joy in his voice. "A true prince!"

The pews rose from the stone floor. Shane only had a flicker of movement as a warning before a wooden bench crashed into him, knocking him backward across the room.

He hit the wall behind the pulpit hard, and his vision went black. Soon, there was only the cold, and eventually, that faded away into the vast emptiness as well.

✳ ✳ ✳

Shane opened his eyes. The world was black. His body was sore all over. He turned his head, and even though he could see nothing, he felt his vision blur. Beads of color and light danced before his eyes in a flash. He felt his head spin and gasped out loud.

He froze in place, holding as still as he could while he waited for the spinning to fade to something more tolerable.

The back of his head throbbed. He let his fingers slide slowly along his scalp until he reached a bruised and sore spot at the back. It felt jagged and lumpy. The skin had broken, and he could feel dried blood and a large, tender bruise. He'd hit his head exceptionally hard.

Half of his body was cold. He was lying on a stone floor. The cellar, most likely. It was cold and dark and silent. The humming of the truck engine was gone. He could only hear his breathing.

After a moment, he heard a drip. Just a single sound, a splatter somewhere beyond his feet. He waited in the stillness until he heard it again, just a little over a minute later. A slow drip from some source, landing on damp stone, but there was nothing else.

Shane braced his hand on the floor. It felt dusty, and despite the dripping he heard, very dry. There was grit beneath him, fine and chalky. He sat up and had to stop again as his head sent him reeling once more. The process was going to be slow.

He breathed deeply, trying to control the feeling in his head, trying to will away the effects of the head wound. He pushed off the ground and eased himself into a sitting position.

Shane's jaw clenched, and he squeezed his eyes shut as if it would stave off the dizziness. It did no such thing, but he fought through it, nonetheless. His breathing was ragged by the time he was upright. He felt tired and sore all over, and he saw lights in his eyes that swayed and pulsed to a beat that mimicked his thumping heart.

He leaned back gently and felt cold, dry, wall on his bare flesh. His clothes were gone. He was exposed and vulnerable. None of it mattered to him right now. He kept his head forward so the wound would not touch the stone.

It took a long time to slow his pulse and breathing. He counted off the seconds in his head and then realized he was rushing his count, matching his pulse, and had to start again. He tried to stay even and measured. He had to stay calm.

He sat still for a long time. Ten minutes. Thirty minutes. He stopped counting sometimes when his mind wandered and then lost his place and started again. The wound on his head was bad, probably a concussion. It was hard to make a self-diagnosis alone in the dark.

The spinning lessened with time. Measured breathing and focus were what he needed, so that was what he did. When Shane was able to move without feeling like he might tumble over, he rose to his feet. It was a slow process, and he did not rush it. It was easier than sitting up had been.

He kept his hand on the wall and ventured forth into the darkness, using his feet and free hand to explore. He found the first wall quickly. There was a door made of wood but no handle. He traced the seams with his fingers, looking for someplace where he could get a grip and maybe pull or pry it loose. He couldn't find any gaps and could get no grip. He pushed on it, but it made his head swim again. He decided to leave it until later.

He continued exploring, passing the door to the next wall and then around to the rear of the room. The far corner was damp. He reached up and could feel the ceiling. Water was leaking through the stone, just a small amount from a source he could not feel. A miniscule crack, he assumed. Nothing he could exploit.

Shane pulled his damp fingers from the ceiling and tasted them. The water had a mineral taste to it but nothing else. It seemed safe enough. Drinkable. He knelt slowly and felt the floor. There was a very small, recessed area in the stone that formed a shallow bowl. But it was not deep enough to scoop water from. He leaned his face down and pressed his lips to it, drinking the mouthful and a half of water it held.

He got up again and continued back to where he started. Nothing was in the room with him. It was a stone rectangle, roughly ten by five feet. It was a prison cell.

Shane eased himself to the ground once more and leaned on the cold wall. Magister had him now. He knew the ghost liked to draw out death, that it was part of his process. That was what he had planned for Shane. Death in a stone cell.

The water was likely there to prolong things. A person could live for weeks with no food, but death from dehydration would come in a matter of days. Magister wanted it to take a long time.

For Magister, the process of making a ghost was one of torture. Shane would not break as easily as the ghost might expect, though. Starvation in a dark room was not going to do the trick.

Something clicked in the dark. Shane's breath caught, and he stayed perfectly still. The sound had come from his right, in the opposite corner of the drip.

He waited, and it came again, a click like a thin piece of metal being bent, or someone cracking their knuckles.

"Need something?" Shane asked.

The cold air swirled from his other side. Not the brutal cold of Magister, just the predictable cold of the dead. Something sharp dug into his thigh. He felt his flesh separate and then pull. It happened in an instant. The ghost rushed past him, tore a strip of flesh from his leg, then vanished into the stone before he could even swing in defense.

Shane cursed, covering the wound with his palm. The section was not even an inch across, but it was several layers deep, deep enough to leave him bleeding. He would have to be faster if the ghost returned.

Time was hard to gauge in perfect darkness, especially with a head wound. Shane quickly gave up on counting. He let his body tell him how long he had been there by how tired he felt. It was imperfect at best, but it was all he could do. He was already tired and sore. He also had no idea how long he'd been unconscious.

He estimated it took somewhere between one and two hours for the drip to fill the shallow dent on the floor. He had emptied it six times when he heard the click again.

Shane prepared himself. The click came from his right, so he turned to his left, ready to catch the spirit. The cut came from above this time, across the top of his right shoulder. Another thin strip of flesh, cut and yanked in a single, fluid motion. He winced and pulled away too late to do anything about it.

So this is it, he thought. Magister's plan was to pull him apart piece by piece. Slowly and painfully.

The next click happened faster. It couldn't have been more than three hours. The ghost went for the top of his foot that time, just beyond his toes. It hurt more than he had expected and stung far worse afterward.

It occurred to him that the click was unnecessary. The ghost could appear and tear his flesh without making the sound. The click was another part of the torment. A small but sadistic addition. A warning that it was coming, but he would never know where it was coming from.

The next attack was much later. He was asleep, so he had no idea how much time might have passed. He awoke with a pained cry. A strip of flesh was missing from his chest. The other wounds all still stung, but the pain was faint and manageable. He wondered how long until one or more got infected.

It had been at least a day. Shane suspected it had to have been that long. He slept fitfully here and there. He drank when the bowl was full. He had turned the corner opposite the bowl by the door into a toilet.

He kept his mind busy reciting stories he remembered, even if only parts. Or bits of old conversations with Carl or James. Anything to keep some kind of focus. It was easy to lose oneself in a place with no stimulation. Or no positive stimulation, to be exact.

He focused on the ghost, and the feeling of the cold before it appeared. The way it attacked. It had all the advantages, but it was choosing to alert Shane every time. There had to be some way to use that.

He'd lost a strip across his back and another on his forearm in the last two occasions. He'd heard the click and felt the movement of cold air as before. He still couldn't outwit his torturer.

Hours passed. Shane sat cross-legged in the dark, leaning forward. He was making himself small. A smaller target meant a smaller area to defend. He listened and waited.

The click came again. Who knows how long it had been? It didn't matter. The click was not important. He stayed as still as a statue.

Cold air rushed at his back, but that was not right. Something was off. He had only an instant to think about it; to go with his gut in the moment. Shane's fist shot out straight ahead.

He smacked into something soft, pulpy, and familiar. The cold sensation of ghost flesh.

The spirit made a sound, and Shane was on it in an instant. His head swam, but he ignored it. He didn't need to see to do this. He didn't need to have balance.

His hands closed over something and then moved quickly. The ghost lashed out with thin, bird-like claws. Shane dropped his shoulder onto it, pinning the arms and reaching beyond the flailing arms. He found its thin neck, and then the head.

"No!" the ghost growled, its voice like gravel. Shane squeezed.

The ghost burst, and Shane rolled to the side. The pain was bad, but he laughed, nonetheless. His head spun like a top, but he forced himself back up to his hands and knees.

"That all you got?" he asked the darkness, still chuckling.

Something in the corner clicked in answer. The next strip came off his stomach.

CHAPTER 25

THE PRINCE

It was not a drip, and it was not a click, but there had definitely been a sound. Shane lifted his head in the dark, feeling groggy and disoriented. He had fallen asleep on his side, stretched out with his feet almost in the water. Passed out, maybe. He didn't remember trying to sleep at all. The constant attacks, the cutting, and the tearing had made it hard to get any real rest.

His tongue felt fat and dry. It had been two days now, he thought. Two days at least. He hoped Ventura and Herbert had escaped. They could have gotten out of town in the fray and made it back to the blockade. If that was the case, then there was probably a team of CDC specialists storming Burkitt in search of bioweapons already. Unless Ventura had talked his way out of it.

There had been a sound, Shane thought, trying to stay focused. A sound that had awoken him.

He reached out in the dark. It sounded like metal. Something small and metallic falling on the ground.

His hands searched the dusty stone, back and forth. He moved, and it hurt, but he ignored it. Minutes passed, and then he felt it. Small and cold and round. His fingers closed on it. A ring. Not just any ring, either. An iron ring. One of his.

Shane sat up, slipping the ring over his finger. He did not understand why Magister would give him a weapon. Still part of the game, he supposed. Part of the torment. It didn't need to make sense; Magister wasn't exactly the poster child for sanity. It was enough that he had it. It could help.

He made his way to the corner with his water source and drank. There was not enough water to keep him hydrated. And without food, he would only get weaker. Every moment he wasted was another moment he got weaker, and Magister's position became that much stronger. He needed to do something now.

Shane got to his feet and approached the door.

"It's time to change the rules," he shouted. His fist slammed against the wood. No one answered. He slammed the door again and heard the echo in a chamber somewhere beyond.

Shane pounded on the door again and again. He threw his body into it, using his shoulders as battering rams. The wood held fast, strong and resilient, but he did not give up.

"You can't wait me out," he shouted. "I'm coming for you. Time is the one thing you don't have."

The door shook. He hit it again. It rattled in the frame and dust fell from the ceiling. Shane gritted his teeth and growled. He slammed the door, punched it, kicked it, and then started again.

"You forgot who I am," he yelled at the door. "You think you have eternity? You're what comes after life?"

Shane laughed and pounded on the door once more.

"I'm what comes after you! I'm what ends you!"

His head throbbed with every blow, but he kept it up. He could feel it loosening, bit by bit. Whatever lock held the door in place was set into old stone. Old wood, old stone, old metal. None of it would last. Shane had already shown that with the house above. He was not exactly a garbage truck, but he would get the job done.

There was no click this time. Cold air filled the space behind Shane, and he turned swiftly, ducking low. He punched and swiped his hand through the darkness. The iron ring hit something. The ghost vanished and Shane laughed but it returned just a moment later.

The cold was different this time, it was closer to the door.

Shane hit out with his other hand and clipped the spirit. Like the first one, this ghost was not expecting a fight. Shane's arm was around it in an instant and he held it close to his body.

"I can pop the head off of every single one of you if that's what it takes," he told the ghost.

"Good luck with—" it began to reply. He forced his fingers into its mouth to get a grip on its head. The adrenaline was already pumping through Shane's veins, and the struggle was brief.

When the ghost exploded, the force sent Shane against the door once more. He heard wood splinter and laughed as he slid down and sat on the floor, catching his breath. He was not going to die in a ghost's stone prison cell.

A rumbling sound rose slowly in the darkness. It seemed to come from everywhere at once. Shane turned and began hammering on the door again. The sound grew louder and Shane hit on the door harder. He punched his fists into the wood until he felt his knuckles sting and bleed, but he did not stop. Magister's plan was slow torture, so Shane had to change the plan. He was not going to play someone else's game.

"Come and stop me," Shane yelled, laughing again.

He just needed to get close enough to Magister to finish him. He'd crush his head like an overripe melon. It would be easy. And fast. No need for one-liners, no big sendoff for the ghost. He'd just break him and show the others that their leader was done and gone. Like the Custodian. Then they could either back off or face the same fate. That was all he wanted.

The rumbling was impossibly loud now. It sounded like he was in the center of some massive machine, deep in the heart of the engine as it thundered onward, but he had no clue what was causing it.

"Shane."

Something cold fell on his shoulder and he swung his fist about. The cold caught his wrist before the iron ring could make contact.

"Shane, it's me," the familiar voice said.

"Herbert?" he asked. He could not see the ghost at all, but his wrist was freezing in the ghost's grasp.

"I came to get you out of here, but we need to move fast."

"You were supposed to leave," Shane told him.

"I did leave. I would have been here sooner, but you gave the cameo to Ventura. I could have come right back to you."

"You would have gotten your other arm ripped off," Shane countered.

"Maybe. Probably. But come quick, we need to go. I'll get the door."

The cold slipped away, and Shane sat still. He heard something click in the door. The wood shuddered and moved, then fell onto the floor beyond.

The light in the room made Shane wince. More fat candles, like in the chapel, burned along the wall of an empty stone chamber.

"Can you stand?" Herbert asked.

Shane looked up at his friend. Herbert's missing arm was conspicuous and made him look very unbalanced. The rest of him looked the same as ever.

"Yeah. Just a second," he replied.

"I don't mean to rush you. I can see you're not doing well, but this is urgent. This is really urgent," the ghost said. "Your clothes are here if you want to get dressed."

"Understood," he muttered.

He grabbed the messy pile of clothing and slipped into them as quickly as he could. His pants and shirt were torn to pieces, but his jacket and boots were still in one piece. He forced himself to his feet and stumbled briefly as he fought to remain steady.

"This you?" he asked, waving his hand in a circle above his head in reference to the rumbling sound that still filled the cellar.

"Agent Ventura," Herbert replied. "This way."

"What's happening?" Shane asked, following the ghost. He led the way out of the chamber and into another hallway like the one that had initially taken Shane to the chapel.

"You never came out after us," Herbert said. "And Ventura said we had to flee. I didn't want to, but he made a compelling argument for an increased chance of success if he was still alive, and I didn't lose any more limbs. So, we ran."

He stopped then and turned back to Shane. Even missing his arm, the bulk of the ghost took up the entire space of the hallway. There was nothing but Herbert there in the dim light.

"I'm sorry, Shane. I really am. I wanted to—"

"Herbert, come on. You lost an arm already. I got stuck in a prison cell. We needed a better plan," Shane said. The ghost nodded and started moving again.

"Exactly what Ventura and I thought. It was not easy to convince local law enforcement to not rush into the town. Luckily, Ventura looking like he'd nearly just been murdered helped the others listen to his story."

"What did he use to top possible biohazard material?" Shane asked with a weak laugh.

They reached another door, and Herbert paused. He gestured for Shane to be quiet and then vanished for a moment. The tumblers in the lock clicked, and the door fell open as Herbert came back.

"He's an accomplished liar," Herbert whispered. "Suffice it to say we had to rehash our old Plan B into a new Plan B. Or Plan C, maybe."

"I don't know what any of that means," Shane whispered back.

"It's fine," Herbert replied. "We're almost out. I don't know where Magister is, but Ventura is waiting for word you're free while he holds off the others. I think you're really going to like this."

Herbert sounded oddly cheerful, and Shane could only chuckle.

"If this doesn't end with someone ripping off more of my skin, I'm probably going to like it. What are we waiting on?"

"Ventura needs to clear the area," Herbert said. He looked out into the darkness again and then nodded. "This is our best chance."

Herbert left the hallway, and Shane followed. The next room had the same cobblestones and pillars placed at regular intervals. Shane recognized it as the first chamber he'd entered after coming into the cellar from the outside.

They walked a short distance more and then turned a corner. Light filled the space, sunlight this time, and Shane shielded his eyes with an arm but kept walking. He could see the stairs in the distance, leading up and out into the world.

"Can you make it?" Herbert asked.

"Yeah," Shane replied.

His body was sore but not that much. He felt a surge of energy that was born from adrenaline or hope or just the desire to get out and smash Magister's head to pieces. Maybe all three together; he didn't care.

Shane ran with Herbert toward the stairs and then made his way up and into the light.

"Ventura!" Herbert yelled the moment they were free.

Shane could not see the other man at first. He could see nothing but the dead town of Burkitt. The roaring of an engine was clearer now, though. Something incredibly large, like the garbage truck but not.

Shane walked a few paces and then turned toward the sound. He watched as one of the largest dump trucks he'd ever seen backed up the far side of the hill toward the wreckage of Magister's house.

"We should move," Herbert said, as the truck grew closer.

The two of them ran from the cellar as the ghosts of Burkitt swarmed the truck like locusts.

CHAPTER 26
SALT OF THE EARTH

Xander Ventura had never driven a dump truck in his life, but that was the least remarkable of his new experiences. He had no idea how he was going to keep his job. That was assuming he survived. Balanced in that regard, it didn't matter much. He'd rather be alive and unemployed than be a dead agent who maybe got a service medal on his casket for dying in the line of duty.

His excuses had mostly fallen apart by now, though he was not without merit for suggesting some kind of dangerous chemical was in Burkitt. There really was something in the swamp. He could talk his way out of it.

If not for the state of his appearance when he returned to the blockade, the other agents on scene probably would have taken him into custody. He had been bleeding profusely from several significant wounds. One ghost had nearly sliced through an artery in his neck, and another had bitten the back of his arm so badly that the paramedics suggested he needed immediate antibiotics and maybe a skin graft. He assumed the wound was sterile since the ghost didn't have real teeth. Not technically.

He told them there was a serial killer cult in Burkitt. What was a serial killer cult? Who cared? It was a Hail Mary play, but it got the focus off what he'd done wrong, enough for him to get patched up and set to work again.

There were plenty of corpses in town, so by the time anyone else set foot in Burkitt, his story would sound believable. As a potential victim who got away, his plan was going to be to play off any errors or misinformation as "heat of the moment" mistakes to be forgiven. All he had to do was survive. And find Shane Ryan.

Herbert pressed him to return every moment they were out of earshot. Ventura had never realized how stressful being the only person who could see or hear ghosts could be. But Herbert managed to convince Ventura of two things. One, that they needed to stop all the ghosts at once, and two, that Ventura needed to be the distraction while he found Shane, hopefully alive.

Herbert said the cellar was large, and there were many rooms and many bodies. It was the only place Shane would be, he said. Ventura had to trust the big ghost. It was his idea to take Shane's armored truck plan and tweak it.

When the FBI requisitioned a dump truck to help investigate a serial killer cult, things happened quickly. People had questions, but they asked them while they were moving. Things got done. It took twelve hours for the truck to arrive.

And the salt came only a short time after.

Ventura had to install the iron plating to the truck once they were in Burkitt. It took longer than he wanted it to, and neither Lucky nor Herbert could handle it to help him. Once he had it outfitted like the garbage truck had been, they were ready to go.

Magister, in his arrogance, once again did nothing to stop them. He must have assumed the scenario would play out the same as the previous run, if he gave it any thought at all.

Herbert left the cab, and Ventura circled the hill. He was to distract the dead for as long as it took. The armor plating did its job well. Ghosts bounced off left and right. None made it inside. His only concern was the time.

Mere seconds felt like hours. He saw inhuman faces, twisted by age and rot and violence, shrieking at him from every shadow and every corner. Nightmares heaped upon nightmares, and they all wanted his blood. He had to keep moving and keep them busy.

Every ghost that Ventura had seen before was forgettable. Normal, even. The worst he could remember was from when he was a teenager. He was in the hospital visiting his grandmother after her hip replacement. She was doing well with it, and it was supposed to be a happy occasion. But he had seen a man in the halls who was twisted with sickness, his skin yellow and covered in sores. He saw this only for a moment, but the image stuck with him for years.

Now, Xander Ventura was in Burkitt. Town of the dead. So many spirits, all broken and terrifying. And this was Shane Ryan's world. This seemed like any other day to him. The man was able to make jokes, for God's sake. How could anyone live like that?

He had known the man for a handful of days. And Ventura was risking his life to save him. It would be absurd if it had not also been terrifying. Shane Ryan was part of something that he had been trying to delve into for nearly his whole life. A world he knew was real even when everyone had told him he was wrong. He was seeing things. He needed medication. But he knew he was right. And so did Ryan.

Shane Ryan's world was not what Ventura wanted it to be. But that didn't matter. It was what it was. So what if it was a nightmare?

"Ventura!"

Herbert had emerged from the cellar. Ryan was with him, climbing out into the light. Ventura saw them from across the rubble. He sighed, relieved to have lasted as long as he had. Now it was time to see if the plan worked.

He shifted gears in the truck, turning the wheel hard to the right and then reversing, climbing up the hill. He watched in the rearview mirror, lining up the truck with the hole in the floor that led down to the cellar.

Ghosts crawled across the truck. Some crawled across others, making their way past iron plates to get closer to the cab. The face of a drowned man, bloated and pale with sagging flesh, appeared at the passenger window.

Ventura stopped the truck. It was time. He pulled on the lever and the hydraulics kicked in. The truck shook as the tailgate opened and the bed lifted, dumping ten tons of salt onto the ruins of the house.

CHAPTER 27

THE PRISON

Shane and Herbert fled the ruins of Magister's house as the dump truck backed up to the shattered remains. The ghosts crawled across the outer surface and Shane could see many of them vanishing and reappearing. The truck had iron plates on it, the same as the garbage truck they'd used before.

"Plan C?" Shane asked.

"Plan B was a good idea, we just made some modifications," Herbert said. He led Shane around the hill.

"They're closing in," Shane pointed out. The sheer number of spirits allowed them to scramble across one another and avoid the iron. He had no idea what Ventura's plan was, but they were running out of time.

"He can make it," Herbert said, stopping to watch. The ghosts were ignoring him and Shane: The truck was their entire focus.

"Make what?" Shane asked.

The truck stopped, its back end just over the ruins. Hydraulics whirred to life, and the bed began to lift. Once it reached the right angle, the tailgate opened, and Shane could finally see what the vehicle contained.

A rush of pure white spilled from the back of the truck, washing across the ruins in a wave and sinking into the hole that was the entrance to the cellar.

Ghosts popped from existence in a snap. Hundreds of spirits became dozens became a handful in a matter of seconds. What must have been tons of salt poured in a tidal wave and filled the cellar completely, encasing the spirits in their haunted items, sealing them away where Magister had stored them like prizes.

Shane had to laugh. It was a preposterous idea, and it worked like a charm. The entire population of Burkitt's dead, entombed in salt.

Ventura appeared outside of the truck and grinned at the other two.

"It worked!" he yelled.

"I think so," Herbert yelled back.

The agent came to join them near the front of the house. Shane could see a handful of shadows creeping away, scrambling beyond trees and bushes. A few had managed to skirt their fate, but they seemed unwilling to keep fighting after what had happened.

The salt would keep most of the ghosts confined indefinitely, and as long as the items remained buried, the ghosts had no means of escape. The property was immensely dangerous, but it could be handled. Somehow, at any rate.

"We should have done that from the start," Ventura said, laughing. He was bandaged in a dozen places, had a pair of black eyes, and looked like someone had maybe slit his throat. Shane was amazed he had survived.

"How did you get out?" he asked.

"They mostly lost interest in me once you were captured, I think. I just kept swinging at anything that came near."

He held up the iron bar and the chain that was still around his wrist to accentuate his point.

"Never a bad plan," Shane said.

"You look terrible," Ventura told him then. "We need to get you to a medic."

"I need a cigarette." Shane let out a tired breath.

"I'll put that on the list. There's a team still waiting outside of town. I bought enough time to do this," Ventura said, gesturing toward the dump truck, "but you're probably going to have to answer some questions about what happened here."

"Answer them honestly?" Shane asked.

"Honestly about the serial killer cult that was operating here and took you captive, yes."

"Sure… yeah…" Shane nodded, taking a mental note of "serial killer cult".

They made their way back toward the dump truck. Shane wondered which of the items imprisoned below their feet housed Magister. They would need to do some sort of retrieval mission. An excavation to catalog and hold every item that was trapped within the salt.

Shane figured his friend James Moran would be willing to help. He'd have the only level of expertise at handling such things to make it safe as well. There was no way the FBI could be asked to do it. How were they going to connect cataloging various knick-knacks with the serial killer cult story?

And they couldn't just leave it. Rain would come soon enough and wash the salt away over time. No doubt James would be excited by the sheer number of items, not to mention the back story. It'd make his year.

Time, Shane thought. Even imprisoned, Magister had time to rely on. They would need to find him, whatever held him, and encase him in lead. Maybe throw him into the swamp where he could spend eternity. Then he might gain a new appreciation for what time was.

Ventura walked around the front of the dump truck to get in the driver's side while Shane pulled himself up on the passenger side, his muscles screaming in protest as he pulled his weight up to the elevated door. He got in the cab and sat, sighing as he leaned back and rested his head.

Seconds passed, and there was no sign of Ventura or Herbert.

"Guys," he shouted out the window.

No one replied. Shane leaned forward and looked out of the windshield. The truck was larger than even a standard dump truck, and the cab was high off the ground. He could see the distance well but did not have a view of what might have been right in front of the vehicle.

"Ventura?" he yelled.

Anxiety built in his gut. Nothing outside moved, and he grunted, carefully opening his door once more. He climbed down from the cab of the vehicle and hit the ground.

Burkitt was deadly quiet once more. There were no more creeping spirits. They had all vanished now, back to their hiding places. Shane made his way around the large front tire to the truck's front end.

Herbert was in front of the truck. He stood between Shane and Ventura, facing the FBI agent. Ventura caught Shane's eye as he appeared and smiled awkwardly. Behind him, Magister stood with his hand around his throat, holding the agent still. His thumb was pressed against the bandage on Ventura's neck, right above the artery.

"I wasn't wrong about you," Magister said. "If anything, this all proves how right I was. What a resilient creature you are."

His voice was thick with admiration. It was more uncomfortable than threats or torture and death. There was something obsessive about it. Creepy, really. Magister was creepy, beyond the violence he committed.

"You're not down in the chapel with the others," Shane said, stating the obvious. Whatever item Magister was bound to, he had stored it someplace else. Close by, he assumed. But elsewhere. Safe from the prison of salt.

"Of course not. You know this, sir. The common soldier should not have access to the inner sanctum. There needs to be a separation. That is part of the way order is maintained."

"Not an issue for you anymore, I guess," Shane said. "Your whole army is gone."

"Not gone. Waiting. This is hardly a permanent prison, and you know I have nothing but time," Magister said.

Shane sighed and stepped to Herbert's side. Magister flexed his hand and Ventura hissed as his thumb dug into the already existing wound on his neck. Blood spotted the bandage beneath Magister's finger.

"We could work out a deal," Magister suggested.

"Could we?" Shane asked.

"Of course. A gentleman's agreement has ended many a war. Likely started a few as well, I'd wager."

"I can't imagine I'm going to like the terms of any deal you come up with."

"Has it not been said that the best deal is one in which neither party walks away satisfied?" Magister asked. He smiled at his joke and Shane found himself somehow liking the ghost even less than he had a moment before.

"What do you propose?" he asked.

"These two friends are obviously close to you. Important. Are they family? Compatriots? It doesn't matter. I could easily use this one and destroy the other, but won't. For you, I will stay my hand," Magister said.

"How generous," Shane replied.

"You have no idea, sir. I have never made such an offer to anyone before. But I will do it for you. They may go in peace, as whole and healthy as they are in this very moment."

"If I stay," Shane finished for him. Magister smiled again.

"Yes. Exactly that."

He was single-minded in his curious fanaticism, Shane had to give him that. Always focused on his goal, even after losing the bulk of his army to a tomb of salt. The salt meant nothing. It was like learning his daily walk might be inconvenienced by rain.

"I see the appeal," Shane said. "I see the upsides and all of that. But this is all from you. I have a counter."

"As you like," Magister said with a polite nod.

"They leave, of course. But instead of me staying with you, I am going to take your head in both of my hands and crush you like an overripe tomato until that preposterously smug smile of yours explodes into the ether, and no one has to worry about your nonsense plans ever again."

"That's one approach," Herbert muttered, keeping his eyes downcast.

Magister's smile never wavered. He didn't bat an eye. Shane felt the disappointment building in his gut and resisted the urge to swear. He couldn't even insult him, couldn't get a single negative reaction. It was infuriating.

"I understand—" the old ghost began but Shane couldn't handle any more.

"Can you just hit him already?"

Ventura's arm shot out quickly, the iron chain around his wrist and forearm smashing into Magister's leg. The ghost disappeared in a blink and then reappeared an instant later next to the single wall that hadn't collapsed during the garbage truck onslaught.

Shane joined Ventura and stepped away from the dump truck, stepping back from and to the side of Magister as he approached them.

"There is no path to victory for you," Magister said.

He was as calm and confident as ever. Shane had hoped he could make the spirit lose his composure and perhaps slip up that way, but he was achieving nothing of the sort. It was rare to find anyone living or dead so immune to being taunted and denied.

"Get the flail ready," Shane said to Ventura.

To his credit, the FBI agent had no questions. The metal bar fell to the ground, dragging a length of chain with it. Ventura held the rest in his hand as Shane stepped forward, closer to Magister now that they were away from the truck.

"There's always a path to victory for your enemy," Shane explained. "It's just that you can't always see it when you're convinced you can never lose."

"We are not enemies," Magister said as though speaking to a child. "The sooner you accept that, the sooner we can return this place to order."

Shane took another step forward, holding one hand toward Ventura with his palm out to keep him waiting.

"Your attack will fail. I know you know this. I know it!" Magister continued. "I have never lost before. I will not lose today."

"You've never lost?" Shane asked.

"Of course not," the ghost replied.

Shane looked over his shoulder at Herbert and Ventura and chuckled.

"He thinks he's never lost," he said before turning back to the ghost. "You died."

"Everyone dies," Magister said.

"I haven't," Shane told him.

He dropped his hand and crouched low. Behind him, Ventura raised his arm and let the chain loose, spinning the iron bar toward Magister. The ghost didn't even bother to defend himself. He didn't dodge or duck or even raise his hands. He smiled his smug smile and let the iron pass through his head, blinking from existence once more.

Shane was already running. The muscles in his legs screamed, but it didn't matter. He bolted the last few steps up the hill toward the wall as fast as he could. His eyes were focused on a nondescript spot on the ground, a section of earth the same as a thousand others. The only difference—the important difference—was that it was the spot where Magister had manifested a moment before. And it was where he manifested again.

They were face to face, and for just an instant Magister's expression was one of pure shock. The ghost reappeared directly in Shane's path. The smug smile was gone, replaced by an open-mouthed look of surprise.

Shock was not the same as making him lose his composure, or admitting to a humiliating defeat, but it was better than nothing. Shane laughed at the ghost the moment before they collided.

Shane slammed into Magister and took him to the ground. He landed hard and awkwardly atop the ghost, but he had no time for finesse. If Magister was able to summon that freezing wind, then the fight was over. If he got his bearings for even a second, then there would be nothing else

Shane could do. Plus, Shane really wanted to show him how wrong he was.

His hands were on Magister's head, holding it tightly on either side. The spirit screamed as Shane's thumbs plunged into his eye sockets. The resistance was unnatural, but not as powerful as it would have been with living tissue and real eyes. For all Magister's strength and power, his spirit body was as frail in Shane's hands as any other.

Shane forced his weight down with all his power. He pushed like he was trying to force Magister's skull through the earth and back into the salt-filled tomb below. He pushed like he was trying to break the old man. Like his life depended on it.

He growled like an animal and wrenched his hands apart, tearing Magister's skull asunder.

The blast was like a bomb. It hit Shane with a brutal force, and he felt it through his entire body. It was never easy when a ghost came apart. It was never painless. But Magister's destruction felt like he had been caught in a cyclone.

Shane flew backward through the air, breath searing in his lungs and pain cascading across every inch of his being. The house's ruins shook and rambled in the earth below. Shane landed hard on the side of the hill as the final wall collapsed, tumbling down in pieces. Every bit of Magister was gone. The house, the town, and the ghost. He had lost.

Time had finally caught up.

Shane's vision swam, and his head spun. He closed his eyes, and the world faded away.

His last thought was how much he wanted a cigarette.

CHAPTER 28

DEATH OF A GHOST TOWN

There was too much light in the room, and Shane winced even before he opened his eyes. He tried to move his hand but found it slow and tethered. He blinked to focus. Machines beeped around him. There was an IV line in his arm.

"This seems unnecessary," he muttered.

"Not exactly. You were very dehydrated," Herbert answered. Shane blinked again to focus on where he was. A hospital room, he realized, and a small one. No one was there except Herbert.

"Everyone still alive?" Shane asked. He was covered in bandages, including across his ribs. His mouth tasted like metal, and there was incessant ringing in his ears apart from the beeping of the machines.

"Ventura's fine. I'm—well, dead. You lived. We won."

"We won," Shane repeated. "Look at us."

He sat up and grunted as a hundred unfelt bruises screamed to life.

"You broke a few ribs. Plus, the dehydration and the infections from all those cuts. And a concussion. And your finger. I think I'm forgetting some things," the ghost said.

"Is that all?" Shane said. "Didn't even lose a body part."

"Funny," Herbert replied.

Shane grunted and held in a laugh. He had forgotten about Herbert's arm and hadn't meant to make light of it.

"You're awake," someone said, entering the room. A middle-aged woman wearing green scrubs came, checking his monitors and the level of his IV and a dozen other things while asking him questions. He answered as well as he could, trying to hurry her along. She left, promising to return shortly with a doctor.

"Are we on the hook for being part of a serial killer cult?" Shane asked.

"I think Ventura has them convinced you were the intended final victim, and that the killer or killers fled because of your bravery. And his," Herbert said.

"Sounds complicated."

"You saving the mom and kids went a long way toward making everyone more accepting of a foolish lie, I think. Everyone's just happy it's over."

"People like friendly lies," Shane agreed. "Much better than ugly truths."

"People can hear you talking in here," Ventura said, entering the room. "They're going to think you're insane."

"I survived a serial killer cult; it's fine," Shane told him, lowering his voice.

"I'll make up an official statement for you and file it, along with a description of the guy who put you in the hospital. I don't think my unit chief is buying a word of it, but the deputy director already called him to thank the unit on behalf of Delaware's governor and both senators so, you know. Gift horse."

"How many cases do you guys solve with complete lies?" Shane asked.

Ventura chose not to answer as the nurse returned with the doctor. They spent too long going over Shane's injuries with him, explaining how long it would take to heal this or that, and other tests they wanted to run. Some FBI agents came in afterward with questions, most of which Ventura deflected.

"I have to get out of here," Shane said when everyone was finished with him.

"You heard the doctor. They want you here for a few days," Ventura pointed out. Shane grunted.

"Can't smoke. No coffee. These are non-life-threatening injuries. No real reason to stick around," he replied.

It was the next morning when Shane opened his eyes again. He was not sure if it was exhaustion or medication that had knocked him out. Not that it mattered. He'd had rest, as much of it as he needed.

Herbert was still waiting in the room. Shane was glad to see him there.

"I think we should leave," Shane said, startling him.

"The doctors—"

"Yeah, yeah," Shane said, sitting up. "I'll worry about that. Go find Ventura, see if he can give us a ride back to my car. I've had my fill of Delaware."

By the time he made his way outside and into the sunlight of a new day, Shane was eager to have a cigarette and something to eat.

Mostly, however, he just wanted to get home.

EPILOGUE

Shane and Herbert walked the length of the road, from the blockade where Ventura had dropped them off to where he had parked his car outside the woods. The agent had offered to take them to his car, but Shane insisted that the blockade was good enough.

He was slow, his body still sore from what he had been through. The doctor had tried to convince him he needed to stay in the hospital, but he agreed to sign papers so he could pack up his things and leave once anything serious had been taken care of. He was conscious and could walk, and that was all he needed. He wanted to be away from Ventura's coworkers as quickly as he could. There was no more need to address stories of the serial killer cult of Burkitt, Delaware.

Herbert was uncharacteristically quiet on their walk. In fact, he had said nothing at all. Shane had managed to get half a pack of cigarettes from one of the state police officers and finished his second smoke by the time they reached the car, doing so in total silence. They weren't his brand, but they worked in a pinch.

Ventura had given back the cameo necklace, and it was tucked away once more in Shane's pocket. The ghost had said nothing about the exchange. He was distant now, which could have had any number of causes.

"I suppose it's all over now," Herbert said before Shane got into the car.

"Yeah," Shane agreed, taking his hand from the door, and remaining outside. "You good?"

Herbert shrugged. He was down an arm, but it wasn't the worst thing that had ever happened to a spirit.

"I thought I'd feel better when it was all done. All *really* done," he said.

"You don't feel good?"

"I feel like we did the job. I'm glad Lisette and the Custodian and Magister can't hurt anyone again. That part is good. It's satisfying, you know?"

Shane nodded and fished out another cigarette.

"It is."

"Maybe it's not what we did that has me feeling… lost, maybe."

"Then what is it?"

"The carnival was my home for nearly my whole life. And then years after my life. It's all I know. But now it's gone. Everyone is gone. I wanted to get some kind of justice for Dash after all these years. And for Bartolomy, too. For everyone. Maybe even for Lisette. I just don't know if that's what happened."

Shane nodded, inhaling slowly, and letting the smoke drift away.

"It's as much justice as you can get in a situation like this. As much vengeance. And it was good. You know they would have hurt more people if they'd been allowed to keep going. A lot more people."

"I know." Herbert sighed. "I don't feel bad for it. I don't feel it was unjust or wrong. I just wonder what the point is now."

"Point of what?"

"My existence," Herbert said. "Everything I had is gone. Everything I knew. How do you do anything after that?"

"I imagine that's hard to deal with. Having to start again."

"But I'm dead. I don't get to start again. I mean, how? Where would I go? I don't want to be like these… things. I don't want to haunt some hospital, or an abandoned house. I don't want to be alone, Shane."

There was a real sadness in the ghost's eyes. Shane pulled the cigarette from his mouth. He exhaled slowly and considered the right words. For all he knew about the dead, he could only know it from the outside. He was alive and content to remain that way. But he had spent a long time with Carl and Eloise and Thaddeus, and the other ghosts in his home. Long enough to know something about what drove them. What kept them grounded.

"It's not like you don't have friends," he said.

"You have been a good friend. Better than I deserved. You nearly died to help me. I can't tell you what that means," Herbert said.

"Just don't make it a habit." Shane grinned.

"I don't want to have no purpose," the ghost said. "And now that we're done…"

He looked at the ground then, and Shane waited for him to continue. He could hear it in Herbert's voice, hear what he was suggesting. What he wanted.

"What?" Shane asked.

"Everyone's gone, Shane. I want it to be over."

"You're not the first ghost who's said something like that to me."

Herbert looked at him over the roof of the car.

"Did you do it for the others who asked?"

"Not a lot of others. I did it once. For a ghost that was in a bad way. He was barely recognizable as a human. Didn't have a lot going for him. You're not in the same situation."

"What do I have going for me?" Herbert asked with a wry laugh.

"I dunno. But if you get in, we can head back to Nashua. I've got a house. Few friends you can meet. You'll fit in."

"How could I fit in?" the ghost asked. Shane shook his head.

"How the hell do you think? Unless you really want me to end it for you right now. If you ask me, I will."

They looked at each other for a long moment. Then Herbert nodded slowly and, finally, he smiled.

Shane opened the door and got in, turning the key to start the engine. Herbert slipped in a moment later, sitting in the passenger seat with all his great bulk.

"Are you sure?" he asked. He sounded like a guest invited for dinner who was afraid he was imposing.

Shane put the car in gear and checked the mirrors.

"Trust me. Carl needs someone to talk to more regularly, anyway. Plus, the sisters would love you, are you kidding? You were in show business; they'll be thrilled."

He pulled out onto the road and hit the gas. The engine hummed, and a breeze filtered in through the windows.

"Sisters?"

"They're triplets," Shane clarified. "I mean, they're a little off, but who isn't? Same with Eloise. She's charming, just don't make her angry."

The drive back to Nashua was long, but Shane took it at a relaxed pace. He stopped for cigarettes and for coffee, and once to grab a quick bite to eat at a diner where the waitress stared at his wounds like he was a walking corpse. By the time they got home, Herbert knew enough about everyone to know their names on sight.

Shane took the cameo necklace from his pocket, unwrapping the fabric that held it, and slipped it into an old jewelry box in the back of one of the bedroom closets, lost among a dozen such boxes where it would draw no one's attention ever again.

Check out these best-selling series from our talented authors:

GHOST STORIES

RON RIPLEY

BERKLEY STREET SERIES
MOVING IN SERIES
HAUNTED COLLECTION SERIES
DEATH HUNTER SERIES

IAN FORTEY

JIGSAW OF SOULS SERIES
CULT OF THE ENDLESS NIGHT SERIES

SUPERNATURAL SUSPENSE

A. I. NASSER

SLAUGHTER SERIES
SIN SERIES

DAVID LONGHORN

NIGHTMARE SERIES
ASYLUM SERIES

SARA CLANCY

THE BELL WITCH SERIES
BANSHEE SERIES

For a complete list of our new releases and best-selling horror books, visit
ScareStreet.com or scan the QR code below!

Printed in Great Britain
by Amazon

50692507R00115